WAITING FOR LEAH

Arnošt Lustig

WAITING FOR LEAH

Translated from the Czech by
Ewald Osers

THE HARVILL PRESS
LONDON

Published by The Harvill Press 2004

2 4 6 8 10 9 7 5 3 1

Originally published with the title *Lea, Divka z Leeuwarden*
by Quartet, Prague, 1992

First published in Great Britain in 2004 by
The Harvill Press
Random House, 20 Vauxhall Bridge Road,
London SW1V 2SA

Random House Australia (Pty) Limited
20 Alfred Street, Milsons Point, Sydney,
New South Wales 2061, Australia

Random House New Zealand Limited
18 Poland Road, Glenfield,
Auckland 10, New Zealand

Random House South Africa (Pty) Limited
Endulini, 5A Jubilee Road, Parktown 2193, South Africa

The Random House Group Limited Reg. No. 954009
www.randomhouse.co.uk/harvill

A CIP catalogue record for this book is available from the British Library

ISBN 1 84343 147 5

Papers used by Random House are natural, recyclable products made from wood
grown in sustainable forests. The manufacturing processes conform to the environ-
mental regulations of the country of origin.

Typeset in Scala by Palimpsest Book Production Limited
Printed and bound in Great Britain by Clays Ltd, St Ives plc

WAITING FOR LEAH

One

"The SS has a soft heart and a hard heart. It's up to you which one I show you."

– Sturmbannführer Karl Bergel,
Great Fortress, Terezín

In September 1944, I was working with a pneumatic drill on the construction of a railway line. It looked as if it would rain any minute. That day, it was a Sunday, I was collecting spikes spilt between the sleepers. I had two buckets, and they were both nearly full. The Germans needed a branch line linking the fortress to the main line. So we were building the track along which, as soon as we'd finished the job, we'd be travelling east from Terezín to Auschwitz-Birkenau – without return tickets. The empty cattle trucks, sometimes with messages scribbled in pencil or chalk inside (*Mana, don't come. We're full up*), would return to be packed full of people yet again. (These scribbles made no sense: *danger gas*.) My work suited me reasonably well: I was receiving a heavy labourer's ration. The weather at the beginning of September was mild, but halfway through the month it broke. The sky above the fortress was blue, the stars shone at night; in the distance to the north were imposing mountains. Who would have believed that the Germans would be murdering the people who worked for their armaments industry, sewing uniforms and splitting mica for the Heinkels, Messerschmitts and Junkerses of their *Luftwaffe?* Who would have wished to kill so many gifted, at least useful, people?

Quite suddenly, on that Sunday, at the edge of a maize field, I caught sight of Vili Feld. He was not alone, but the moment he saw me he was.

"Going to rain," he said.

"Looks like it."

"Funny, the places we meet." Since he had last seen me, more than a year before, I had grown taller and filled out a bit.

"Lousy weather," he went on, making sure our conversation didn't grind to a halt. "Worse to come. But we'll manage. We're tough."

I gathered his mind was elsewhere. I tried to read in his face what he was trying to read in mine. He had circles under his eyes and slightly thinning hair above the high forehead of his narrow skull. He had a few more years under his belt than me, and (like the rest of us) was living in the ruins of a world that was falling apart without ever comprehending it. Our consciences were all on the line. We had to struggle to gain the slightest advantage, and even then nothing was certain. The ghetto, comprising the Great Fortress, was divided into rank-and-file and important prisoners, with countless gradations in between. The madhouses were as crowded as the hospitals, the old people's homes, the former barracks, the living quarters, the schools and all the workplaces connected with transport (who knew where to?), supplies and maintenance. Instead of the original 5,000 inhabitants, there were now more than 60,000 packed into this place. (The institute for the mentally ill was headed by Heinrich G., the head physician of the Am Spiegelgrund clinic in Vienna, who was busy creating a pure race and had earned commendation by killing 7,000 mentally retarded Austrian and German children. Their parents were informed that the children had died of pneumonia.) Once when I'd walked past the lunatic asylum in the former Kavalier barracks, the patients had been singing:

"Alle meine Entchen
schwimmen auf dem See . . ."

What united us all was that we were waiting for the war to end. Old scores had been buried under a heap of subsequent events. (I imagined the languorous eyes of little Ruth Winternitz, whom Vili had seduced away from me back in Prague.)

The weather was capricious. The wind and rain, which normally came with the onset of autumn, provided an additional hardship. The Czech gendarmes had tightened their security. Vili wore a waterproof coat, wellingtons and a woollen scarf. Even if I hadn't known that he was a big shot on the construction project, I'd have realized it from what he was wearing. He carried no tools, no shovel, pickaxe or hammer. I glanced at his hands.

"How long have you been working on the line?" he asked.

"Five days. And you?"

"Two years." He grinned. "Everybody finds something to do here. Things could be a lot worse."

It started to rain.

"Never stays fine for long." He looked at the sky.

We had run into each other at the edge of the maize field

because I had needed a pee. He had been standing there with two women, one a tall blonde (quality sheepskin, quality furrier work) and the other hatless, with wet, lanky hair, an overcoat and a circular brooch on the lapel of a red woollen suit. Both women looked nervous, as if they hadn't slept, and sad. Around them were wet straw and rotting leaves. Broken stalks and maize cobs. Mud, gravel. Behind us were dug-up land, scrub, twisted metal, sawn-off lengths of rail. The rain fell on all this.

The women handed Vili a waistcoat with contraband sewn into it. There wasn't much time to observe them. The maize field gave them cover. They left the moment they heard me. I probably scared them off, or maybe they had concluded their business. I heard the rustling of the tall maize as they pushed their way through. Vili and I were alone. I knew he was a chess player and normally planned five moves ahead. (He had always been like that and probably had no choice in the matter.) There had been a look of panic in the women's eyes, of fear, helplessness and resolution all at the same time. Vili threw the waistcoat over his left arm. I tried to guess, as quickly, what it might contain. Eggs? Flour? Sugar? Cigarettes? My mouth began to water. German marks or British or American money? All kinds of things were being smuggled into Terezín and traded there. Here, too, the man without fear survived. He who risked more lost less, unless of course he lost everything. He who took no risks blended into the shapeless mass about whom no-one cared. The mass of the confused and disorientated who didn't know anyone. I waited for Vili to say something to me.

"If you help me with this, it'll be worth a hundred cigarettes to you."

In the distance the women were hurrying away. We could

hear the final rustling of the maize. The rain swallowed up the sound. I wondered if they had spent the night in the fortress. I didn't know where Vili was living. It wouldn't have been the first time that women separated from their men had come into the fortress for a night, or for several days, and then left again, despite the danger. Some women in mixed marriages amazed their men by their steadfastness, their disregard of the obstacles, and they probably also amazed the Czech gendarmes charged with fortress security, and even the Germans. Other women just disappeared as if the ground had swallowed them up. Mostly they were non-Jewish or half-Jewish women without religious beliefs, or girls whose parents had divorced. Some would bring food, others – for a few hours – themselves. The value of the sacrifice outweighed reason and risk.

"How long were they here?"

"Not long," he answered evasively.

"Did they spend the night?"

"Not this time."

"Did you hide them inside?"

"Not this time," he repeated.

"Hope I didn't scare them too much. Or scare you."

"Not this time," he smiled into the rain. He was a little nervous, which he wasn't as a rule.

Swallows settled on the harvested part of the field behind us. Now and then they would fly up into the rain, so low they almost darkened the sky. The sky was like glass with milk poured over it. Had the women come to encourage Vili to escape? Had they offered him a hiding place outside? That was the most remote possibility. A few "submarines" had remained in Prague and in the countryside. If the Germans caught them, it meant the rope or the axe. It occurred to me that the women might be hiding among the maize, waiting for me to go away.

"The cigarettes are in the waistcoat," Vili said.

Cigarettes equalled money. Like gold or precious stones. It was always the same with Vili. There was always something I couldn't explain. His eyes looked sore. Was it lack of sleep, or the rain?

The maize field had swallowed up the women. It was bucketing down now. Why hadn't Vili made a move yet? Our presence might still endanger the women, just as theirs might endanger us. There was no shortage of German inspections of the railway line. I thought of one of the women's swollen ankles. I didn't envy them for having to force their way through the wet maize. For the previous seven days, the fortress had been strangely quiet. Then the Germans had executed seven men for writing to their families outside. Then they had hanged another nine. Others were executed in the Lesser Fortress for offences less grievous than meeting a woman. They'd had a visit from an Aryan mother, lover or friend. Or they'd sent greetings home on a postcard, adding that things were bearable here (two football leagues, lectures by VIPs from Europe, an occasional ticket to the cabaret. A little more food wouldn't hurt).

It was still pouring, I found it difficult to speak. The water was bubbling between my lips.

Now, Vili threw the waistcoat over his right arm. He was leaner, more muscular and probably more self-contained than he'd been in Prague. His grey eyes, which held you like a third hand, were searching my face. I knew he could manage to get the waistcoat inside by himself. I'd got involved in this business by accident.

6

It was Sunday, an extra shift; we were alone. I was trying to imagine how he thought of me: as uninvited guest or witness? For him everything was a trade-off. Through no effort of my own, I had the advantage. The soft, reddish clay of the raised railbed appeared luminous in the rain. The rails shone as did the sleepers. It would take just a few more weeks to complete the construction work. The German engineering experts already saw themselves elsewhere.

"They seemed to know what they were doing," I said. "Impressive."

"In 30 minutes they should be there," he said.

I gathered he meant the railway station.

He looked at his watch. Was the risk worth a hundred cigarettes? I hesitated. How much was a lot when the alternative was the rope? The Lesser Fortress, from which no-one returned? Transportation to the East as part of the Nazis' "final solution", which, for the moment, we were postponing by our stay in Terezín? It occurred to me that it was a miracle that we weren't all of us singing *"Alle meine Entchen"*. Why should I help Vili, even if I'd be helping myself as well?

He didn't look bad, with that waistcoat over his arm, although he was wet despite his raincoat. There was about him the air of a man who knows how to cope. That was a quality of his, not a virtue. In the glittering of his eyes was that bit just before the finish line, just as it had been in Prague, at the Hagibor sports ground, when he had won the 1,500 metres. Or when he had seduced girls half his age. Had he got used to the idea that he could get away with anything? Had he brought it with him to the fortress?

There were fewer SS guards and Czech gendarmes about

on a Sunday. The SS left the day of rest to the gendarmes so that they could earn the favour and trust of the Third Reich. The Germans went all spiritual on Sundays in their *Kamerad-schaftsheim*. They'd listen to Wagner and, in the evenings, to Peter Kreuder and his orchestra. They'd down their beer and sing *"Trink, trink, Brüderlein, trink"* or *"Ein Heller und ein Batzen"*. They were noisily cheerful with their "Hai-li, hai-lo". The Germans believed that the Czechs were better off than they deserved to be. The Germans didn't see too much of a difference between the Czechs and the Jews. Meanwhile, they let the Czechs manufacture tanks, aircraft and shells by the million.

The field was becoming sodden. The sky was oppressive. The birds skimmed through the mist and rain.

"We should get the hell out of here," I observed.

Swallows were flitting overhead with their bluish wings and white bellies.

"Yup," he nodded. He was giving the women time. We could no longer hear them.

I inhaled deeply. It was high time for us to make a move.

We were both wearing the wellingtons we'd been issued. I took the waistcoat from Vili. He helped me off with my jacket so I could put the waistcoat on. I did up all my buttons.

"You've put on weight," he smiled.

"Yes, for once," I said.

We set out on the path to the sentry box. We both had signed workmen's passes with the right rubber stamps.

"You just hang on to the stuff, I'll do the talking," he said.

I was getting used to the waistcoat. It was quite heavy.

"Two are more likely to trip themselves up than one."

"Whatever you say," I agreed.

The swallows were circling round us.

"I don't know the gendarme on duty today," he said. "Let's hope he's one of the good ones."

He spat into the mud. When we talked, the water got into our mouths.

"Who'd choose to be on duty on a Sunday?"

"My thoughts exactly."

"I wouldn't put my money on any of them."

"Neither would I," I remarked. "Let's hope for the best."

We splashed through the puddles. In addition to the waistcoat, I was carrying a bucket of spikes in each hand. My eyelids were glued shut by the rain. The mud was deep. Every step was an effort. We trudged along. I was wondering about the gendarme. It poured and poured.

"I can see the barrier," Vili announced.

The little hut and the barrier appeared through the rain. Water ran down them.

"Let me do the talking," Vili repeated.

The wind was creating watery curtains. The rails and the railway bank were being tested. (More German engineers had arrived from the Reich, representing the Deutsche Reichsbahn.) If the bank collapsed, they'd say: Jewish work. If it survived the weather, the credit would go to the German supervisors. To Hauptsturmführer Heindl. To Commandant Rahm from Vienna.

"Still got your mascot from the Hagibor?"

"I was parted from it in the canteen."

"Our people?"

"Gendarmes."

He found it difficult to speak in the rain.

I felt the tension in my stomach. I imagined he felt the same.

By the barrier stood the hut of the Czech gendarmes charged with guarding the Great Fortress. The Lesser Fortress, the political prison – everything was politics to the Germans during the war – was the responsibility of the Waffen-SS and the Prague Gestapo. The gendarmes were a mixed lot. They included old regulars from the First Republic and reinforcements from the Second. By guarding factories and similar installations in the Protectorate of Bohemia and Moravia, they saved the Nazis men for front-line service. The warriors of the Reich were thus able to fulfil their tasks in the West and in the East.

"It's the hut where I'm on the list," I said. "But probably a different sentry."

"Let me walk in front of you."

I thought of the Lesser Fortress, where prisoners were made to stone their fellows who'd tried to escape or committed an offence. Sometimes the Commandant's three daughters would watch. It was either or. Either you stoned your fellow prisoners to death, or you went to the gallows yourself. It had never happened that prisoners had not stoned their condemned comrades to death. For those three girls, the Commandant, their father, had had a little wooden balcony built, like a box at the theatre.

Inside the little hut stood a sergeant with an emaciated face, acne and a lined forehead. He was looking out of the window. In front of him was a list of names already ticked off and a sharpened yellow pencil. I was prepared to overlook my prejudice against people with bad skin. I studied him like a lunar landscape. Would he let us pass? He could, but he didn't have to. What would he take from someone he caught smuggling? He was alone. He wouldn't be afraid that we would grass on him.

My gaze hung on that pencil. How long had it been since I had had anything in my hand that would write? Education was not encouraged in the fortress. It was enough if Jews could count up to a hundred, the race experts declared. To be able to read and write was unnecessary. On one facet of the pencil I saw *Koh-i-noor* in small letters. The name reverberated in my head. Vili wore a poker face. Focused, seemingly calm, though not carefree. It occurred to me that this was how gamblers looked when they were concentrating, or workers when they sat down to dinner. To men his look suggested masculinity; it brought out what was most feminine in women. What response would he elicit from the sergeant? I thought of the two women in the maize field.

The game had begun. There was no turning back. Would the glint in Vili's eye catch the sergeant's interest? Hadn't it once hypnotized me? In the air hung the threat of deportation to the Lesser Fortress or to the East. How should a person who had nothing play against one who had everything?

The sergeant's expression was like an egg that had to be cracked before one knew what would emerge. The sergeant knew more than I would ever know. About letters smuggled in and out. About who had been arrested and what had happened to them. He'd have his opinions about risks worth taking, about what was stupid, treasonable, advantageous, suicidal. About how quickly or slowly people lost character or courage, about what point they'd break at. He seemed to me like a football referee who didn't care who won or lost, but who knew the score. The Nazi machine was indecipherable. It followed a different logic from that of its victims. The Nazis would twist the most mundane things into secrets. They turned hatred into action whenever it suited them.

We both knew the gendarmes didn't kill. They merely reported back to their superiors and to the Germans, who then decided the nature, place and time of the punishment. The gendarmes were a telegraph, the text of a telegram.

To neutralize my fear, I played a mind game children play. I wished the sergeant everything good if he let us pass and everything bad if he detained us. The sergeant was silent. We were creatures from two different planets. What was he thinking about? The race laws of the Third Reich? What Hitler had in mind for us? It was impossible to know. Did he realize that, in the eyes of the Germans, the Czechs had no business being in their own lands? Shouldn't he feel closer to us than to them?

Why was I having to depend on the invisible worries, disappointments and demons of people I didn't know? How, I wondered, had the sergeant behaved at school? Did he have sisters or a brother? He could have had secret Jewish ancestors – that had frequently been true of Czechs since their defeat at the White Mountain and the Catholics' victory over the Protestants centuries before. How often had conquerors of the Czech lands changed the inhabitants' shirts, coats and souls? I had no choice but to use my imagination. I wasn't well educated enough to know about the Celts and the Teutons. (That came later.) I concentrated on the long yellow pencil and the list of names partly ticked off and partly not. On the sergeant's ruddy face, his green uniform, his black leather boots.

Was he aware of the advantage he had over me? He probably was.

The sergeant was in his forties. His skin was coarse, his eyelids were swollen. A receding chin. In his eyes was a gendarme's experience. I tried to guess what kind. How many people had he got into serious trouble? How many had he helped? His irises reflected Vili's face.

His uniform with its ribbons, stripes and green cloth was reminiscent of a peacock. Of a tropical bird. Gold buttons, a belt. The rain enhanced and simultaneously reduced their gleam. He shifted his weight from one foot to the other.

He had a round face. Inquisitive eyes. There was in him a trace of what the Czechs had been telling their children for a thousand years: We've got to serve the superior force. They've humiliated us, we've been occupied. All we can do is keep our heads above water. No point in bashing our heads against the wall. Got to do what they tell us to do. Lie, twist the truth, humble ourselves, deny ourselves. One day you will be able to speak the truth without inhibitions. Except that future generations still had to tell this to their children when they grew up. Did the sergeant have children?

I could see the wet, shiny signposts: Litoměřice – Prague, Pilsen – Karlovy Vary. We were 62 kilometres from Prague. Those signposts were our only link with the world. The sergeant had one foot here and the other over there. There were worse things than serving in the gendarmerie.

Whoever said that Terezín was purgatory, a pre-hell, had no idea of hell's many layers. (Ourselves included. We were not yet in Auschwitz-Birkenau, in the Warsaw Ghetto or in Treblinka.)

It was still pouring with rain. It occurred to me that a frog might leap out of each of the sergeant's eyes. I prepared myself to say that I had nothing on me. That I wasn't carrying anything. I hadn't done anything to anybody. I hadn't killed anyone. (As if that would be enough.) I was ready to lie my way right into hell if only I came through it alive. Any lie was more justified than the noblest truth. Lies at least gave me false hope. Given the risk, it would be better to lie for all I was worth.

I was holding the two buckets of spikes. I wished the sergeant had had to walk through the mud with that load. In addition to the spikes, water had collected in the buckets. What would the gendarme want to know?

Vili and I were both wet through by then. I didn't put the buckets down in the mud: I wanted the sergeant to think he should have a look at them. He could search right down to the bottom. There was nothing under the spikes. Would he want to look? I would hold on to the buckets until he told me to put them down.

The sergeant came out into the rain. He soberly sized me up. He asked what I was carrying. He looked into the buckets. In his eyes was the expression of people who had learned to say something different from what they were thinking and who were expecting others to do the same.

The sergeant wasn't bothered by the rain. It was blinding me. On the hut was a notice in German: *Ghetto Theresienstadt. Festung. Eintritt strengstens verboten.*

"Now what do we have here?" the sergeant wanted to know.

"Spikes, sergeant." I was alert.

"Nothing forbidden?"

"Nothing, sergeant," I lied. I tried to sound matter-of-fact. I could hear my own awkwardness. But perhaps he would believe me.

It was impossible to guess what the sergeant was thinking. His Sunday was spoiled, and would have been even if it hadn't been raining. He was bound to know by now what fear, hunger and hopelessness did to people. We were living in an empire of fear, where each little spider was afraid of another, and even of itself, of its own web and the flies caught in it. Fear penetrated and enveloped everything like some invisible poison gas, and on top of that there was hunger. The sergeant had already lived through a few frightening changes. He stood there in his high lace-up boots, his shins protected by waterproof gaiters. (One foot in the mud.) The skin on his hands was coarse and spotty. I tried to think of something more mundane than whether I might face flogging, a firing squad or a noose round my neck. Transportation to the East didn't seem so terrible. There would still be a journey before the punishment. We didn't know how long this journey was or its destination. Or what might happen en route. I could feel my heart beating faster. I hadn't realized I was such a wimp.

Through the window of the hut, I could see, on the sergeant's desk, the list of names, the yellow pencil and, behind these, a daily paper, the *Express*, and some field glasses. On a little table were a packet of cigarettes, a box of matches and an ashtray with a few stubs. Across from them was the greasy paper wrapping from his lunch. Had the sergeant had bread and lard, or a ham sandwich? Or liverwurst? Had his wife sliced him some onion rings? In my mind I could smell something roasting. I swallowed.

The wind was blowing the rain against the sergeant's back and splattering against the hut. The rain got into my eyes, as it did into Vili's. The sergeant was in no hurry. On his brownish lips was a tiny screw of tobacco, and his teeth were yellow from nicotine. He turned to focus on Vili.

"Nothing forbidden? No contraband?" he asked. "Nothing to sell inside?"

He had a croaky voice. The corners of his eyes and mouth were moist. Rainwater ran down the deep grooves on his face. Why did he ask? Surely he didn't expect an answer.

"What's it like inside?" the sergeant croaked. "Anyone waiting for you?"

"The Block Elder, sergeant."

"So?"

"We're a bit late."

"Everything as it was?"

I couldn't tell what the sergeant meant. He had his own vocabulary. Different tones for different words.

"It's tolerable, sergeant."

"Hitler is sending some important Jews over the age of 65 here. Decorated front-line soldiers from the German Army in the First War. You've still got some big cheeses among you."

His words were drowned in the rain. The mountains and the vast plain beneath them were lost in the mist and streams of water.

"History's given you a beating more than once," the sergeant went on. "History has ambushed you repeatedly. You've already got a lot of experience. You're used to it. We aren't."

Then he said: "Everything they threatened you with has already happened. We don't know what's in store for us yet."

Was this an accusation?

I didn't mind the sergeant not paying attention to me for the moment. On the contrary. Had history given us a beating?

Had the beatings not always been administered by human hands? Next he would accuse us of being nomads, at home nowhere, as if that was our fault. How often I had heard this from non-Jewish friends – innocent prejudices with far-reaching consequences, things they had heard from their parents. Weren't a thousand years in this country long enough to be settled here?

What did looking at Vili or at me make the sergeant think of? What had he been spared thanks to his mother, his race or mere accident? I would have had to have examined his head with X-rays to find out, just as he probably wanted to examine Vili's.

"Your destiny is already decided," the sergeant continued. "You know where you stand. We can't say the same. They've counted you. How many are there of you, as a matter of fact?"

"Sixty thousand, roughly, sergeant," Vili answered. "The Commandant's office has the precise number."

"Ten times as many as when I started here. What was that postcard they found with the nine they hanged?"

From somewhere in the distance came the sound of thunder and a lightning flash. The sergeant's eyes slid down the barrel of his rifle. A shovel was leaning against the hut. There was another flash of lightning. The thunder that followed it dispersed. The rain was creating curtains and, nearer to us, prisms of light. The sergeant could be sure that no-one could hear us.

"Lots of half-Jews? What about mixed marriages?"

"Apparently, they haven't yet decided in Berlin what status to accord to half-, quarter- or eighth-Jews, or sixteenth-degree ones for that matter. It will mean a lot of divorces. '*Mischling*

17

ersten Grades' is what half-Jews are called, officially. One brother might be inside and the other still at home."

The sergeant was interested. "Suppose someone's got a Jewish ancestor, say from back in the Crusades?"

Vili shrugged. He smiled, politely. "I wouldn't venture that far back, sergeant."

"What do you drink?" the sergeant continued. "They say the water isn't safe. That could be disastrous. I heard that alcohol was being smuggled in. Cigarettes, tobacco and drink."

"That I don't know, sergeant. It's possible."

"I remember the black market back in Prague. It's spreading here."

It seemed to me that the sergeant knew what questions to ask.

"The place is emptying out," he said a bit later.

Streams of water and wind blended with his words. The rain splashed into the puddles and mud.

"Not many of you left in the countryside. How many of you were there?"

"Three hundred and fifty thousand, sergeant."

The sergeant gazed at the mountains. "Are you expecting to be moved?" He didn't wait for a reply. "You didn't want to come here, but you don't want to leave either."

Nobody said anything.

"Lots of your people gave their nationality as German in the 1936 census."

"Nationality wasn't an offence, sergeant. The Jewish question, or the German question, or the Czech question were just questions of statistics."

The sergeant said slowly, "There's a lot of gold inside. Heaps of money and good stuff. A hell of a lot of precious things."

It occurred to me that his words had a shadow. Or teeth and claws, and blood. Some kind of invisible whip. How words can be a trap, a trick and a net, not for butterflies or birds, or lions! The things that start with words and end in bloodletting. The things that words promise.

"Probably not as much as people outside think, sergeant, nor as much as some of us might wish," Vili added. Smiling must have cost him. I had the impression the sergeant was circling round his objective. He had a whole orchestra of voices inside him. He seemed like a bird of prey, circling high up and suddenly pouncing as a mouse emerged from a hole. Two mice.

"Is life expensive inside?" the gendarme asked. It sounded like a double entendre.

"We had to hand over anything made of gold to the Prague branch of the Reichsbank, sergeant. As far back as 1942. What people bring here they use up in no time. It's a bit like living out of your wallet, sergeant."

"You gave up everything?"

I was still wearing the waistcoat. My muscles, my wrist and finger muscles, hurt, and I had bellyache. Would I faint? I had to hold out a bit longer. I recalled that beneath the fortress there were hundreds of kilometres of catacombs, passages leading God knew where. It was damp down there, but it wasn't raining. They had been built a century and a half ago by 140,000 workmen who had taken ten years to do it.

Another flash of lightning and thunder at the foot of the mountains. The rain was getting heavier.

"Some people inside have hideouts, connections to the outside and long arms." A moment later he asked: "What do people take with them to the East?"

"What they stand up in, sergeant," Vili replied. "We follow the Boy Scouts' motto 'Be prepared'. A small suitcase, a box. That's all they allow. They say that if we need anything else, they'll supply us with it later."

"And what happens to the rest of their clothes?"

"The Commandant's office sends them to the *Winterhilfe*, sergeant."

"You parcel the stuff up yourselves for the Germans?"

"Yes. Clothes, footwear, sweaters. Underwear. Accessories. Leather goods. What's left of fur coats. Gloves."

Vili spoke into the rain. He had to hold the gendarme's attention without arousing his suspicion. It occurred to me that I could put my buckets down, but I tried to convince myself that I might suggest to the sergeant that he should let us go now. Vili was trying to do the same thing.

"The *Winterhilfe*, hmm . . . So you're not that afraid of us?"

The wind was bending the sheets of water. Was the sergeant saying these things out of boredom? Did he accept us as he did the pouring rain? Or did we seem strange to him despite the fact that we communicated so easily in the same language? Did he see us, as the Germans did, as people without a homeland, as the refuse of the most varied nations who were now being transported to the East just as they had been sent to Terezín? He couldn't be unaware of what the Protectorate radio was saying, of what the newspapers claimed every day about the circumcized ruining of the world.

I thought about the waistcoat. About the fine line between safety and disaster. About why even the tiniest things can have enormous consequences. And about how little life is worth.

The sergeant said: "You've got some VIPs inside – the

Austrian general Sommer, the French naval minister. The former Czech Minister of Justice, Meissner. I'm told that a quarter of those inside have converted to different faiths."

"Didn't help them much," Vili argued, as politely as he could.

"Probably not," the sergeant conceded. "But a member of the International Red Cross was impressed by it in June. D'you think the world will let such people down? Foreign radio stations broadcast appeals that the Chief Rabbi of Berlin shouldn't be harmed. Is he on the Council of Elders?"

"He sweeps the road," Vili said. (My friend Adler and I had worked with the rabbi on the sweepers' team. In the mornings he'd drive a hearse with bread and coffee made of roasted acorns, or with coal, to the bakehouse, or timber to the joiner's shop. He swept the roads to avoid being put on the council. He didn't want to be on it. He felt cleaner in the dirt of the road. They made him an honorary member, nevertheless.)

"You've got connections everywhere. A thousand years and the whole world, that's quite something."

"We're cut off from the world, sergeant. Things are changing all the time. We just wait by our suitcases." Then Vili added: "For us it's always five minutes to twelve, sergeant."

"Everybody knows about you. That means they also know about us, if you follow me. How did that visit by the Red Cross go? They say the Swiss delegate stayed half a day."

"Old women washed down the pavements. The road was repaired. Bricklayers plastered the façades. The children were coached to say 'SS Uncle Heindl, SS Uncle Rahm, are we having sardines again for supper?' Teenagers were given tickets to hear the Meyer-Sattler duo play German dance music at the café."

"I heard about that."

Vili was silent.

"Is the head of the Council of Elders a rabbi? Is it true people call him Murmelschwein? D'you know him?"

"By sight."

"And his wife? She's not a day over 20. Said to be a Hungarian Jewess. They say a lot of women offer themselves to him. How did he become so prominent?"

"He wrote two volumes of Jewish history, was a successful functionary in Vienna, talked regularly to the Gestapo."

"He's a fatty," the sergeant said. "Seen him a few times. Didn't look to me like a rabbi, a historian or a ladies' man." Then he added: "You people are like sheep."

(This remark remained in my mind for a long time. In our place would he have done differently? Weren't the gendarmes also like sheep – except when they were ordered to be hyenas or wolves?)

At that moment I did feel like a sheep, a shorn one at that. It occurred to me that the sergeant saw us as cattle awaiting the slaughterhouse, just as the Germans did. Except that he spoke our language.

We didn't like Murmelstein. Did he collaborate with the Germans more than was necessary? Nobody knew exactly how much he was forced to do, nobody could weigh it up, and nobody could tell what someone else would do in his place. The council heads before him had been executed by the Germans. It was said that he had an outstanding memory.

"I heard his lecture on Josephus Flavius."

"Who's that?" asked the sergeant.

"A Jewish general. Commanded a Jewish fortress in the war against the Romans and surrendered. Let himself be taken prisoner along with the last few survivors, after most of the defenders had been killed. In Rome they gave him Roman citizenship – as they did to others – and let him write the history of the war." He tried not to make it sound like a lesson.

"Shit," the sergeant said. "And what did his contemporaries say? I bet a few heads rolled." Then he went on: "So long as there are human beings, there'll be lots of things that don't make sense."

My arms were getting numb. My knees were beginning to give. More thunder and lightning. I had heard that the Swiss commission had been accompanied by two new SS officers from Berlin, Roland Scheidegger and Eugen Ringfeder, both of them *Sturmbannführers*. Oberführer Horst Sismondi acted as the French interpreter. My friend Adler had got these names from a secretary in the Council of Elders.

"When you're told to get a thousand people ready for transport to the East, you get – under Murmelstein's leadership – two thousand ready," the sergeant said. "From the allocations for the fortress your leaders save a wagonload of flour a month and send it back to the Reich. It said so in the gendarmes' circular."

It was quite true. The Germans had handed the ghetto economy over to the Jews. And fixed matters in such a way that we had to do the worst things ourselves. We couldn't know what extremes this was going to assume in Auschwitz-Birkenau, where Jewish *Sonderkommandos*, selected from newly arrived transports, would drive their own people into the gas chambers, their own mothers and fathers, until fresh *Sonderkommandos* would take over, and so on, in six-month cycles for the duration of the war. The man who'd been scrimping the German allocations for more than eleven months was called Friedmann. He knew that so long as he made those economies, he'd be postponing his own journey east. The more flour and coal he could save, the longer they would take to replace him. The Jewish leaders' zeal was understandable but inappropriate. They were feeding the fairy-tale dragon either with princesses or with flour. They were in charge of old people's homes, hospitals, crèches for mothers who'd given birth on the way from Berlin, Copenhagen, Amsterdam, Prague and Florence. They wanted to prove to the Nazis that their experiment in self-administration was a success. They were trying to be useful to Germany.

"There are two sides to everything," the sergeant observed. "Or three or four. In a way you're lucky. The question of which side you're on has been decided for you. Not so for us."

Vili realized the sergeant was testing him. But not in philosophy. The sergeant shoved his hands into his pockets. His questions were feeling Vili all over like a doctor's examining hands. Where he discovered fear, he'd probe deeper. There's fear in everybody, for each person a different fear in a different place. Except where everyone's fear is the same.

"It would be interesting to know how much gold there is inside and how much money – ours, German, any other." The sergeant had reverted to his previous subject. "And how much dynamite."

Vili was still standing to attention; the rain was running down his neck. He was aware of the ambiguity of the sergeant's questions. Of what wasn't being said. With his arms hanging down, he looked like a boxer. He reminded me of the time we had done some boxing at the Hagibor, to prove to ourselves how tough we were. Now I was thinking only of the buckets.

Of how a man might suddenly lose his strength even if, a moment earlier, he'd prided himself on it.

"Much of the stuff hidden here will remain so when this place in emptied." The sergeant pursued his line of thought. "No-one will know where anything is. Nothing'll happen to the gold. The dynamite will get damp. Money will cease to have value. Except British, American and Swiss money. Isn't that a pity?" He shifted his weight to his other foot. "It might be worth searching this whole warren, 219 buildings on more than half of a square mile. Metre by metre, lodging by lodging, loft by loft and cellar by cellar. Who knows what's been left behind, sewn into the clothes of people who're already gone? In tooth-paste tubes, in the heels of shoes. Behind beams or under the floor or behind bricks."

Vili remained silent.

"Been here long?"

"Two years, sergeant."

"A person learns how to handle himself in two years. You're bound to have a lot of experience. What's lost is unlikely to be found again. A pity."

Vili kept his mouth shut. Was the sergeant done with us? I concentrated on the list of names and the pencil inside the hut.

"I'm watching you," the sergeant continued, wiping his nose. "You talk, but you aren't saying what you think. I'm listening to you, but I'm not hearing much."

He sighed. It changed into a wheeze. It sounded like an accusation and a warning. There was no understanding in it. His lips produced a sound that could mean a hundred different things. People aren't born smugglers. They become smugglers. Gradually, with experience, they become masters of disguise, schlemiels out of necessity. I thought how secure the sergeant must be feeling in his uniform and strong boots. He didn't have to worry about where he didn't belong. He didn't view the world as a broken watch. No problem for him to get wet through, knowing that in a hour, or two at the most, he'd be dry.

"It must be the way I'm asking," the sergeant said. Where did smugglers rank on his scale of values?

The principal sound now was the cawing of crows. I tried to imagine the racket if I dropped my buckets. Is there somewhere a book of destiny, as religious people believe, a record of your good and wicked deeds that writes itself? I tried to imagine myself in a fairy tale. Should I ask for God's help? If it helped, why not? But our God wasn't recognized by the Germans, and even the most religious of people had found it easier to take Him seriously in better times.

"How many people are still at your worksite?"

"I think we're the last ones, sergeant," Vili answered.

The sergeant blew some raindrops off his lips. Maybe he wanted this to be over.

"Are you sure?"

"I'm responsible for the site, sergeant."

"I've heard that you have visits inside from girlfriends, wives and friends. Sisters, wives or whores." (I was reminded of my father telling me about the prostitute Gallows Toni, who, in Egon Erwin Kisch's story, is sent to the cells of those sentenced to death. But it is by her own wish. In the Lesser Fortress, a wife crept into her husband's cell – both of them were prisoners. They shot the husband and beat the wife to death. They had a son in England. A pilot in the RAF. It was still possible to smuggle people in – through the kennel. They got out again

26

through the gendarmerie gate. Inside they'd have a yellow star stitched to their clothes, once outside they'd rip it off. People also had trysts by the River Ohře and by the slaughterhouse. There was always someone with itchy feet, making things more difficult for the rest of us. The Reich forgave nothing. But some people won't keep quiet until they've got their fingers burned. And they don't care if someone else gets theirs burned as well.)

The sergeant exhaled heavily into the wind and rain. His breath had an echo. He lit a Vlasta. He puffed little clouds of smoke into the rain. He spat out a screw of tobacco. Did he want us to take a message into the ghetto? Or was he telling us what was possible?

The handles of the buckets were cutting into my palms. I wondered when I'd get cramp and have to give in. It seemed to me that a large white animal was flitting through the rain. I was hungry, I was cold, and things weren't looking too rosy. Was it affecting my mind? I thought of the German telephonist from the Commandant's office. She'd ride round the fortress on a horse, her long fair hair flowing behind her. The officers would photograph her. Rumour had it that she was the mistress of the Commandant, Dr Siegfried Seidel. And that a new officer from Vienna was after her, one Anton Burger. Burger had killed 20 sick Jewish children with a shovel; he shot people for the slightest offence. For stealing a lump of coal at the railway station, a log, a potato or a piece of bread. He would stand on the ramparts or on the bastions. Then I recalled the German Jewish VIP who'd been given a room in the Magdeburg barracks, a room with a washbasin but no lavatory. So he urinated into the basin. It was said that he had two doctorates and artistic ability. Just as someone else might press a four-leaf clover or a rose petal into a diary, he was said to have had a pubic hair from the German singer Zarah Leander. The pain in my palms was getting worse. I focused on the sergeant's boots. What mattered to me was to pass muster in Vili's eyes. In my own eyes. In the sergeant's eyes. I wanted Vili to know more about me than just that I had grown taller and filled out a bit.

In front of us were the ramparts. Brick, originally red, now faded and crumbling. Even in the rain and mist, one could see the whole fortress from here. Bastions and trenches from 150 years ago, when the Austrians were still afraid of Prussia, from the days of horses, syphilis and howitzers, of dreadful sewers and the Empress Maria Theresa, who, it was reported, could be aroused by a horse's penis and didn't like Jews, whereas her son, who succeeded her, liked them quite a lot. (He restored to them the rights his mother had deprived them of.) I felt I couldn't hold those buckets much longer.

"Got any money on you?" the sergeant suddenly asked Vili.

Was he starting all over again?

"Unfortunately, no."

"Food, alcohol, cigarettes?"

"No."

"Medicine?"

"No, sergeant."

"No gold?"

"No."

"Nothing that might interest me?"

Did he mean reading matter?

"Unfortunately, no, sergeant. Or maybe fortunately. Not this time."

"Nobody brought you anything?" The sergeant became thoughtful. "Maybe you can tell me some news from the ghetto that I don't know? What about all those European actresses and singers? What about free love?"

I didn't need to remind myself what there was in my waistcoat. It included my hundred cigarettes. I had the feeling I was losing something I'd never had.

"D'you know where most of the trains go?" the sergeant asked, suddenly.

"There's talk about the East, resettlement and normalization."

"To Dresden," the sergeant said. "Cracow. The Auschwitz plain."

Vili didn't say anything.

"Heard about it?"

"Nothing definite."

"Got to be a huge settlement, considering all the trains that have gone there already. And they all come back empty. Germany's acquired a lot of new territory. What d'you suppose they do with them there?"

"There's supposed to be gas works, textile mills, furniture workshops. Machine sheds. There's talk of factories being built, of schools and farms. Of opportunities for work and making money. Starting a family. Some transports carry machines and tools. Some consist only of workers up to the age of thirty."

"Have you heard the term 'final solution'?" Then he asked: "How come so many of your people stayed here as if they were rooted to the ground? Why didn't they leave while they had the chance, the time and the money?"

"Family and friends, I suppose. Property. The knowledge

that they had lived here for generations. Hardly anyone thought it would come to this."

"You could have been in America, in England, in Australia," the sergeant said. (He probably didn't care what the weight of those spikes was doing to me.) "Your time in this country has come to an end. The Germans will do anything to make Europe *Judenrein*. They've got you just where they want you."

Vili did not reply. He didn't say that people applied for visas in vain, or that not everyone who wanted to emigrate had the money to do so. The sergeant had asked about virtually everything that Vili was thinking. What grown-ups and children inside the ghetto were constantly guessing about. The sergeant knew what was what.

Next he asked: "Is another transport leaving?"

"We don't know."

"How long since one left?"

"We've been waiting. They never keep us waiting long. They want it to come down like lightning. We're sitting on our suitcases. It's always the quiet before the storm."

The Germans tried to make sure the transports to the East coincided with Jewish holidays. Most people went off on Yom Kippur. Even the Council of Elders only learned of the dates at the last moment. The Germans were fond of organized haste. Chop, chop, before people realized what was happening. Everyone was afraid of holidays. In this way the Germans killed two birds with one stone.

"Nervous already?"

Vili guessed what he meant. This was different from travel anxiety. Did the sergeant know something we didn't? Was this a question or a bit of information?

"If they ordered you to die out, you'd die out," the sergeant said.

"We're more like Wiener schnitzel, sergeant. Thinner and thinner."

"Schnitzel? More like roast veal!" the sergeant corrected him.

Even though the time between transports was anything but calm, every transport upset established relationships. The Germans were playing a simultaneous game of chess with the fortress's 60,000 inhabitants. And they were several moves ahead, decisive moves. They had a plan, tactics and a strategy. The inmates of the ghetto could only guess. Promises meant threats, threats had a touch of promise about them. No-one could see the cards the Germans held. They were forever changing them. They were excellent players. And they held all the trumps.

"Here at least things are familiar," Vili said.

The sergeant was right: sooner or later, the fortress would be *Judenrein*, purged of Jews. The word reverberated between my temples. Few languages have so many composite nouns as German. Where would the sergeant be posted when they finished with us? Did he think they had put him into a gendarmerie uniform by the grace of God?

"You've got a classy prison," the sergeant said, finally. "If you are schnitzels and they pound you, you shouldn't complain. Those who've already left aren't as well off."

"Who wouldn't rather be here than out east, sergeant?" Vili agreed, politely.

"Dammit all," the sergeant said. "We got martial law for Heydrich's assassination; you get curfew and lights-out. That should tell you something."

31

That SS dandy Heindl would ride into the fortress on his grey. He got the first Jew he met to hold his reins. "Gently, a horse isn't a pig, *du Schweinehund*." He found it laughable that anyone should be afraid of his horse. He'd lend his grey to the blonde from the Commandant's office.

Burger would drive through the ghetto on his tractor. It was known that he wouldn't stop for anyone. We were under permanent martial law. They never let us forget the contempt in which they held our lives. To them Jewish blood was only water.

If I were a gendarme, would I have wanted to kick someone who was already down? Make someone with a sprained ankle run? Make a man with a torn-out tongue cry?

"Something's cooking," the sergeant said.

What was he alluding to? Why was he dragging this out? What was he really up to?

"You probably know what happened to the head of the Council of Elders, Epstein?"

"Only rumours, sergeant."

"They shot him in the Lesser Fortress." Then he said: "He had a woman friend. What happened to her?"

Vili remained silent. She had left on a transport along with Epstein's wife. The sergeant must have known what he was talking about. How could this bit of news have escaped the ghetto? It had been thought that Epstein had been imprisoned. Did we know so little compared to the sergeant because we didn't want to know everything? We scarcely knew more about our leaders than we did about ourselves.

All three of us were soaked through. The sergeant sighed. It struck me that he resembled a parrot. Why was he playing games with us?

"What can you buy inside the fortress?"

"Mustard," Vili replied. "Clothes made from cellulose. And we can buy coat hangers."

"Got any ghetto money on you? Or you?" He turned to me. I shook my head. "We're in the same boat."

At last the sergeant gestured towards me – but not to let us go. (This I understood instantly.) He made me raise my arms. I put down my buckets. It was a relief, even if I was frightened. Wordlessly, the sergeant began to undo my buttons. While he was questioning me, he looked me over carefully. It was obvious that even while he had been speaking to Vili he'd not forgotten about me.

I was wondering whether Vili and I would hang together or whether they would beat us to death. Would they order the older prisoners to stone us? In the Lesser Fortress the Germans were even executing their own people, decorated front-line soldiers and officers, deserving men from the First War. Would they send us east? That seemed the better alternative.

The capaciousness and contents of the waistcoat surprised the sergeant.

"I know a couple of types like you."

It was still pouring.

Without us, neither the Germans nor the gendarmes could feel as important as they did. It was enough not to be Jewish for the sergeant to have all the superiority in the world.

It occurred to me that the Gestapo might pick up the two women at the next train stop. I did what I could not to feel sorry for myself. At least now my arms felt better.

The sergeant had arthritic fingers with a signet ring. On his face were fine purplish veins. His back was ramrod-straight.

He'd finished his cigarette and thrown the stub into the mud. Raindrops were splashing against the hut and his cap. Water ran down the shovel and the butt and barrel of his rifle.

The waistcoat contained Van Houten cocoa, a tin of Nescafé, a bottle of Alpa embrocation, paper tubs of caramel, flattened to get more of them into the two tails at the back. All things which, due to shortages, had increased in value tenfold. The waistcoat hung down as far as those warm linings that Germans and Austrians have inside their waterproof coats. It also contained cigarettes, a 20-dollar bill, a brochure on art by André Breton and Leo Bernstein-Trotzky, eau de Cologne, sugar, soap, tea, salt and dried mushrooms. All in double-stitched linen bags with white drawstrings at the top. The two women had taken a great deal of trouble. That, I thought, was love.

"Sugar, coffee, perfume," the sergeant said. "You have the ghetto in your hands at night. So now you want it in the daytime as well?"

He was met with silence.

"Is some woman involved in this?"

Should I say I had found the waistcoat lying in the maize field? Denounce Vili, or he me? If I said something quickly, Vili might stick to the same story. If the sergeant kept everything, we might escape with our skins. We wouldn't complain to anybody. Once more I was gripped by terror. Of the Lesser Fortress. Of transport.

I told the sergeant my mother had met me in the maize field. (I could hear my voice. That awkward tone. That matter-of-fact tone that suggested indifference.) I felt puny. I was ashamed of myself.

"I've got eyes and ears," the sergeant said.

There was no similarity between us and the people in the Jewish fortress that surrendered to the Romans, who then made them Roman citizens. Nor the suicides at the fortress of Masada in ancient Israel, who after a heroic resistance preferred to kill themselves rather than surrender.

"Button yourselves up, both of you. And beat it," the sergeant said.

I felt like a person who'd been drowning and could fill his lungs with air again. I looked at the sergeant's wrinkled skin, at his parrot-like uniform. At his lips brown and cracked from smoking. Did he really mean it?

Vili also couldn't believe his ears. Or had he expected this? His grey eyes brightened, and his poker face softened. Did I admire his sang-froid? I found myself blushing. A hot wave rose up in me before a chill ran down my spine.

The sergeant said: "I was on guard duty in Lidice before they executed all the men and levelled the village to the ground. They moved the women and children into concentration camps in Germany and Poland, and they transported the horses, cows, goats and chickens here."

"I was involved in burying them," Vili said. "We all wanted to get it over with as quickly as possible."

"Us too," the sergeant remarked.

He picked up his rifle, which he'd rested on its barrel so rain wouldn't run into it. His eyes still reminded me of a parrot's. Not until later did it occur to me that a person's appearance doesn't betray much.

"Be off with you," he said. "And don't run into a German patrol. Or into my boss, Janeček. If you do – forget it."

His voice was matter-of-fact again.

I buttoned up the waistcoat and my jacket just any old how. The sergeant watched me with sleepy eyes under their bluish lids. Suddenly, his little moustache didn't seem so neat to me.

"I smell blood," the sergeant said. "Never before have I smelled so much blood." And finally, maybe only to himself, because his words were hardly audible in the rain: "We'll all meet in hell."

I grabbed the handles of my buckets. They no longer seemed so heavy. I'd have been able to carry them to the ends of the earth.

"Drop that big carton of Camels," Vili said to me.

"Come back, you've dropped something," the sergeant called out.

We walked on. Vili didn't look back. We didn't know if he was watching us. It was still raining heavily. It thundered again. The wind carried the sound away to the mountains.

The vision of the two women came back to me. They had no idea what they'd just escaped – thanks to an unknown sergeant. Thanks to Vili or me. Sometimes it's a good thing that we have no idea of the danger we're in.

"If the Gestapo had caught those two women, they'd have been in deep trouble," I remarked.

"It's always like going for broke."

"Apparently," I tried to agree.

"Last night I dreamed of railway engines."

Things suddenly made sense.

It was still bucketing down.

"D'you know what it's like to stand around holding buckets of spikes?"

"You'll be okay."

36

"Sure."

"I know Gottlieb Faber on the Council of Elders; he claims that the greatest part of the universe is invisible. Know what I'm trying to say?"

"Not this time," I teased him.

We had quite a distance to walk yet.

"Lightning doesn't strike twice – or not in the same way."

Had this kind of thing happened to him before? He'd seduced my girlfriend, little Ruth Winternitz, before we left Prague. I'd not forgotten that.

"Sometimes I'm almost glad I'm here. Not for the bad things. Maybe you know what I mean."

"Yes," I said.

"I've met people here I probably wouldn't have met elsewhere."

Nobel Prize-winners for mathematics, medicine, circumcized men, presidents of famous European universities? I probably underrated the importance of acquiring knowledge before they could bump me off like a dog. The fact that in addition to the Milky Way there were billions of galaxies in infinity, of which I was a part. Or that the Japanese imperial family was the longest dynasty in history, going back 124 emperors and 2,550 years, all the way to Anteras, the goddess of the sun. They'd been wearing the same cut of silk kimonos for 1,200 years. So what? It was all the same to me. I was looking after my own skin. Was Vili thinking of his mother? Or his father? Or his little sister who had vanished somewhere out east, none of whom he ever mentioned?

"I heard Hitler on the radio. That's enough for me."

Vili took one of my buckets. That was a relief. We walked

along L Street and down Q Street to the Firemen's House, close to which Vili had a small attic with a dormer window. He was a second- or third-class VIP. He'd reached that position thanks to Gottlieb Faber. On this inferior level he shared his favour with former generals and senior government officials. We passed the abolished Catholic church with its tower and clock. Once a week, accompanied by a Waffen-SS NCO, the clock was wound by a Czech clockmaker from Litoměřice. I watched Vili's face. Was he thinking of the women on the train? What, I wondered, was his relationship with them? Who else was involved in this business? Did he simply not think of the danger he was in? The Germans had wound our world round their little finger, knowing they could do anything.

"I feel like a French aristocrat."

"Not because of me, I hope?"

"You know how to handle situations."

"I try."

"With my head on the block."

"At least we aren't bored."

"That's for sure."

The streets ran up and down and across. The ghetto was surrounded by walls and ancient ditches; these were filled with rainwater which stank. New water was added to the stagnant water. In the old days the soldiers had filled the ditches to stop attackers. We passed the bridge over the Ohře, and then various streets, blocks and houses. A former mill. One of the buildings used to house a brewery and a still. Later – about a hundred years ago – the army administration had turned the inn into an officers' mess and, right next to it, so the officers couldn't be seen and didn't have far to walk (and no-one was shocked), a brothel. There, 39 prostitutes enjoyed the best of all worlds. It wasn't a big fortress. It had the shape of a stone star. The streets were half empty. No-one took any notice of us.

"The purest expression of our existence is prostitution," Vili said. "False understanding. Pretended elegance."

Did it occur to him that I might run away with the waist-coat?

"Life's a fraud," he added.

"Sometimes," I admitted.

"Even if everything's true."

About that time, we learned later, the Nazis liquidated the inhabitants of two small towns in Silesia – Sosnovice and Bedzina – in the gas chambers of Auschwitz-Birkenau, from the first infant to the last old man, because they found a firearm on somebody. No-one survived. In occupied Poland, German SS *Einsatzgruppen*, Sections A, B, C and D, were on the rampage and ultimately killed one and a half, if not two, million people. They mowed them down at close range, children, old men, women. They made the men dig mass graves and finally shot those who shovelled earth on top of them. That was the beginning of the "final solution" of the Jewish problem. What at that time was still called resettlement or normalization. *Entjudung*. What we in Terezín were waiting for. In relative comfort.

I was thinking about the sergeant. Walking with just one bucket was easy. I switched it from one hand to the other. The gendarme was gradually disappearing from my consciousness. I relegated him to his world and forgot about him. (I was reminded of him later when the Germans executed 14 gendarmes from the fortress for helping Jews.)

"Thanks." Slowly, with the back of his hand, Vili wiped his lips and swollen eyes.

"Last time I felt so good was in Italy on Isola Bella," he exaggerated.

We were both soaked through and had mud up to our knees. As muddy as the fortress itself.

"What can I do for you?" he asked.

"What do you mean?"

I could work in his squad if I wished. Laying rails. Did he want to fob me off with a promise instead of what we'd agreed on?

He invited me to his attic. It was only a bit further on.

"My rabbi grandfather used to quote Maimonides, the healer of body and soul: 'Anything I did yesterday was bad, and tomorrow I'll lose the certainty I had today.' I usually decide what to do and then immediately forget it after doing it. Man is a little ripple on a river, breaking over the bank."

He took a deep breath and spat the rainwater off his lips.

"I've already forgotten," I lied.

We were still walking along L Street, past the former manège, which now housed the joiner's shop. We turned into narrow Q Street and, a short way from the Kavalier asylum, into an even narrower lane until we stopped outside the building where Vili lived with about a hundred other people.

The old sparkle had returned to his grey eyes. He again seemed to me to be a cat with nine lives. Perhaps I was as well. Perhaps we all were. Time would tell.

"I don't like looking like a drowned rat," I said.

Suddenly, it seemed as if it wasn't rain on his face but sweat. Was he thinking of the two women? Would they come another time? Was I jealous of him? We'd moved a bit closer to one another again. It was a ludicrous alchemy. Friendship and hostility. For as long as I'd known him, everything had always come out all right for him. He simultaneously proved something to me and disproved it. What could anyone still do for him?

"You can't predict the future," he said.

"You're reading my mind."

"You can only play the hand you've been dealt."

The wind was blowing from the fortress. Everything was wet. The red-brick buildings with their low roofs were lashed by the rain. New mud joined old mud. It was getting chilly.

Two

"In an unsettled age, we wish our guests peaceful days and hours in the new year."

– New Year's card from the Commandant of
Auschwitz-Birkenau, Christmas, 1944

The furnishings of the tiny attic – two flimsy partitions and one brick wall, beams, a dormer window and a chipboard desk – betrayed a feminine touch. "Leah," he said, and introduced me.

"How did it go?" she asked.

"No complaints," Vili replied.

He didn't mention the women in the maize field.

"Was it dangerous?"

"You know what it's like."

"I'm learning," she said.

"It's over for now."

She smiled, furrowed her brow and moved towards him. It occurred to me that their vocabularies were similar. She'd probably copied hers from him.

"I don't like being on my own. You should take me along next time."

"You'd want that?"

"Almost."

The first thing that struck me was how pretty she was. I

breathed in her girlish perfume. Not to mince matters, I was bowled over. She was beautiful. A porcelain complexion, young and fresh, a perfect body, barefoot, a loose top of pale blue towelling and a white linen skirt made from a tablecloth. I'd never been so close to such a beautiful woman before. My heart was racing, but differently from before. She had a well-proportioned face, a slim figure, an alto voice and skin like rose petals. She was looking at me attentively if perhaps a bit uncertainly. I could hear noises from next door, the building's noises. She had golden hair and pretty hands.

She shifted her weight before coming towards me and extending her hand. Her skirt clung to her belly and thighs and for a second outlined her crotch. The sense of her body pervaded everything. I just about managed to take in her face, her hair, her breasts, her eyes and her sex. I was afraid I was blushing. I had the feeling that I was gobbling her up. I took in her voice like a caress. A mixture of recognition, disdain and irony. There was something in it that she'd overcome, something that had been there a moment earlier and that she'd got rid of. She accepted my presence as if she'd expected it. It occurred to me that she was not fully aware of how beautiful she was, although she must have known what it meant to people like Vili Feld. (Or to guests.) She had a friendly handshake. Did she hold my damp hand in hers for an extra moment? Her animal warmth flowed into me. Suddenly I felt I had known her all my life.

"Are you always in such a hurry?" she asked.

I didn't understand.

"I'm impatient," she said. She didn't have to add that she'd been imagining what might have happened to Vili.

It was still pouring outside. She kissed Vili on the lips. It was a nice kiss. Her kiss, too, involved her whole body. In her kiss and on her half-opened lips there was something more complete or older than she was herself.

"You're sopping wet," she said. "These past few days even the weather's been against us. You've no idea what it means to me when you come home, when you bring something with you and when you're all in one piece – hands, feet, your head on your neck."

This was appreciation. The appreciation of a woman for the man who provides for her. I thought I could understand their relationship.

"I wish I could be more courageous. So you could take me with you."

"You don't have to be that good. So long as you're careful."

"I'm not even careful. You two are like gladiators."

She had arrived in the winter of 1942 on a Dutch transport from Leeuwarden via Westerborg. Two years ago, I calculated, she couldn't have been more than 16. Westerborg was another imitation existence intended to prepare people for what would happen to them later in the East – the underground undressing room, the bathhouse with the showers that did not spray water. Westerborg was another town created by Hitler and Goebbels and Himmler. An imitation of self-government, including Jewish officials, architects and economists who were allowed to function so long as they served German interests. That was the first place where brother didn't know brother, never mind how they acted or what they believed. A wedge driven by the Nazis into the Jewish community, which had already become unstable because it had no hinterland.

"It's hard to lean on a chair when the back's disappeared. Isn't that so?"

"We're all acrobats. We don't need chairs to sit down."

"I am impatient," Leah said. "I'll have to work on myself."

She stretched out her arms. I was trying to orientate myself. Again, her smile held something older than her eyes or her face.

"Some things I haven't yet learned to wait for, and others I haven't yet unlearned to hurry for."

Did she bleach her hair? Where would she get bleach here? My tension from the encounter with the sergeant was yielding to one of a different kind. I tried to find something in her to dislike. I was slowly overcoming my embarrassment. She was so pretty. To me she suggested someone who had one foot in yesterday's world, a world I could scarcely imagine any longer. How had she got hold of Vili? Where had Vili met her? She ran her fingers through her hair. Her hair, her lashes and her brows were like flax. Small ears, a straight nose and large expressive blue eyes. Her unwrinkled skin suggested thick milk or cream. With her long legs standing barefoot on the stone floor. In the corner was a pair of wooden clogs without heels. It occurred to me that she was naked under her clothes.

We began to get out of our coats and boots.

"You took a while, but it's all right now," she said. "I'm a nervous Dutch Jewess," she smiled.

"Those are the worst," Vili grinned.

"I like it that you know me so well."

"Of course, I'd rather come home to you in one piece than not at all."

"I don't like being panicky, I'm sorry," she said. "Sometimes my eardrums feel like they're going to explode in the silence. A few minutes seem to me like ten years."

"Everything's fine, darling," Vili said.

"I'm glad you think so."

"That's what you have me for, isn't it?"

They were all smiles. He spoke to her differently from the way he'd spoken to the sergeant or to me. His self-assurance had returned; there was certainty in his voice. Perhaps this was false elegance or exaggerated calm, but it banished her misgivings. The glint in his grey eyes. She was looking very girlish, if not exactly carefree.

"It's over for now," he said. "The sergeant at the hut told me a few things. I admitted to him that we don't have the most reliable news here. It comes to us through too many filters. He remarked that we were dying out."

"That's what they said about blondes in Leeuwarden."

There was something else in her voice now. I could imagine how she'd cling to him, a feline smoothness in every movement.

During that fraction of a second, I intuited something between a passing relationship and one of another kind. Perhaps this was an echo of the two women in the maize field, of Vili's other women whose existence or proximity Leah sensed and from any guilt for whom he already had absolved himself. This was one of the rules of life in the fortress, where everything was temporary. Nothing could be assumed to be enduring.

Her voice was pleasant, even though it was a little tense. "I feel this is a language I don't understand."

"I don't know if it was worse this time because we're worse, or if it will be better next time because we'll be better," Vili said, with a smile. "Or because it depends on others. The worst thing is that we never know."

"I'm getting more tired all the time," she said.

"Aren't we all?"

"I shouldn't admit it to myself."

"No, you shouldn't."

"You'd probably like me less if I did."

It struck me that they were clever. I liked the way they talked. In my world nothing was free. I preferred people who were good, people I didn't have to be afraid of.

"Isn't life like ju-jitsu?" Vili smiled. "Until they count us out, with both shoulders on the floor, or we count them out. One round after another."

Leah handed us two towels from a box by the wall. Above the box was a shelf with books. (That was a real luxury.) They had a pre-war German introduction to philosophy, a volume with Freud's name on the spine, a few novels and story books in French and German and some fat old periodicals. I knew from back in Prague that Vili was fond of reading. Once at the Hagibor he'd recommended Josephus Flavius's *Jewish War*. (That's why he'd mentioned it to the sergeant.) In Prague he'd lent me a novel about New York, *City for Conquest* by Abel Kandel, the child of Romanian immigrants, which had been read eagerly by half the orphanage.

I dried my hands and face, the wet under my chin and on my chest. Then Leah handed Vili his dressing gown and me her own.

"I hope it's not too small," she said.

"Looks a perfect fit," I said.

Vili made a screen from a heavy blanket. He suspended it

from hooks in one of the beams. We could change behind it. That's a good start, I thought. Vili looked more muscular and thinner than at the Hagibor some years earlier. (Again I thought of little Ruth Winternitz. Had his adulthood attracted her? His elegance and assurance? What had he liked about her? It all came down to instincts. These were my unsettled accounts. We could compete again, even though it would be in secret. This was only the beginning of an idea. Was I thinking of Leah as the prize?)

"Darling," she said again, "I'm so glad you're back." She stroked his face with both palms. "I'm not the bravest person in the world."

"You know my rule: Never accuse yourself."

"I could do with some good news."

"Aren't you better off without news?"

"My mother wanted me to become an actress."

"It's never too late," said Vili. "My rabbi grandfather wanted me to become a dentist."

In her voice I heard helplessness or the contempt women use as armour. I wondered how she'd been feeling before he got back, alone, aware of the risks he was taking and also of that other alternative – that he might not return and she'd never see him again. This had nothing to do with marriage. Or with selling one's body. With the morality the world had known since the Flood, before the camps and the fortress. She also knew what the punishments were, and that people did not return from the Lesser Fortress. (Or, if they did, beaten up and about to be transported to the East.) She exuded a femininity I couldn't name. A strength present even in a girl's weakness. She was talking to me and to Vili as if we'd known one another for ages. Did she have bruises on her arms? They looked like bruises. Where – and how – had she got them? I'd only just noticed them.

I told her my name. And my address: L 218, Boys' Home, Room 16.

"We're old friends from Prague," Vili said. "We met by accident. The way people meet here."

"You didn't know you were going to meet?"

We preferred not to answer that one.

"You've got to change," she said from the other side of the blanket. "Each day I meet fewer people I know," she added. "People are here today and gone tomorrow. The day after tomorrow you'll say that only the day before you saw someone who no longer exists. He stays in your memory for a split second and then vanishes. I don't mean to be morbid."

"You're going the best way about it," Vili said through the blanket.

"So many have left."

Vili was still undressing. Everything we had on had to be wrung out.

Old people were making a noise on the other side of the door with its iron hinges. Part of the building served as an old people's home. I tried to ignore the sounds, but it wasn't easy. The house was full of them. I could visualize them crowded together, bedbugs, mould, stench. Suitcases ready, tied up with string, for all eventualities. The old people's home had been set up by the Council of Elders two years earlier.

From the Commandant's office came a *Sondermeldung*, a special announcement, preceded by a Franz Liszt flourish. It floated up over the fortress. Then came the news, the words all running together, impossible to make out.

I took off the waistcoat and handed it to Vili. He put it on the bed, the largest item of furniture in the room, which he'd covered with paper. Even Leah's freckles added to her beauty. Under the dormer window I saw a small box with a pot of cosmetic cream wrapped in margarine paper. (It occurred to me that the women in the maize field, who'd smuggled the waistcoat through forbidden territory into territory even more forbidden, had had no idea who would share their cargo.) Was I pleased by what Vili had said about our being old friends?

Again she seemed to me like a china figurine come to life. Was she making herself look older because she was so young? On the wall I spotted a mirror in a wooden frame. I studied her reflection in it. The fortress had taught me not to under-estimate creature comforts. What was older in her than her actual years? I thought of something that would enable me to square accounts with Vili. We were almost the same height. We could be rivals. Something in Leah was calling out to me: Don't be afraid – of anything. Or maybe something was calling inside myself. The damp was overwhelming. My stomach was growling. Why was I feeling guilty when I hadn't done anything yet, except in my mind? Perhaps I had a fever.

"Was there any difficulty at the barrier?"

"We got through," Vili replied.

"Thank God," Leah said.

I was wondering what kind of girl Leah was, to find a protector with connections to someone who could fish out the card with your name on it from the index box, so that someone else would go on the next transport to the East instead, because – that was German law – someone had to go. Hardly anyone would be put off by the price or by thoughts of their reputation. The limits of sin were called into question. Self-preservation excused nearly everything, even if hundreds of voices insisted otherwise. Anyone who, in the beginning, when the *Aufbau-Kommando* transports, the AK1 and AK2, arrived, the ones that set up the ghetto, claimed that honour and character retained their weight even here was a liar. Or a wishful thinker.

"There's always some difficulty," Vili answered. "Sometimes there's confusion. It's hard to steal when even your host is a thief." He laughed at his own words. "There's no lack of confusion," he went on. "You never know anything in advance."

"Same people as last time?"

Her pupils reflected her matter-of-factness as well as the rain and the streaks of low cloud. She knew something about his transactions. (Not everything.) Had Vili brought me with him to let me see who was sharing his accommodation, or to get me out of the wet, or so that Leah should see that the transaction with the waistcoat involved trousers as well as skirts? Again I realized how pretty she was.

"When I'm waiting and you don't come it tears my soul apart, just like when my father used to take me along with him when he bet on horses. I'd hate to end up wearing mourning clothes."

"Don't worry about me. I do what I can."

Considering that it was raining outside and the window was open, she wasn't wearing much. How had she got her bruises? Had she had a fall? Had someone attacked her?

On Sundays the Germans left the Terezín ghetto alone. It was unlikely they would call Vili back to work, but it couldn't be ruled out. Leah closed her eyes. It occurred to me that she was acting like somebody falling asleep or just waking up.

Bedroom eyes? Her face, the way she walked, her speech – the impression she made. A painting on which light played. (Later she told me that she was sensitive to light and darkness like animals and bugs are, or like some people are to the weather.) The sound of the rain changed into a vision of her skin becoming moist under her clothes. I saw in my mind the building that once housed the still, the brewery and, later, the officers' mess with the brothel next door. That, too, had been made into an old people's home. There were more elderly people here. The younger ones were being assigned to labour transports going East or to Germany. With the old people they didn't have to worry about rebellion. (One labour transport, a thousand men, had returned from Germany. They told us how Allied raids were wrecking the country. They were taking the war back to where it had started. The Germans in Germany, the men said, were more humble.)

The old folk next door made themselves heard again.

"They know what's going on," she said. "There's no great joy in getting old," she added. (I didn't yet know how to apply this idea to myself.)

It wasn't possible to make out what the old people were arguing about, except for the German word *verschwunden* – "disappeared" or "lost". In terms of culture and memory, they were more German than anything else. The Nazis had thwarted their plans. They had Jewish blood. Their ancestors had not sprung from German soil. The Jews were Germany's misfortune, Julius Streicher had written in *Der Stürmer*. They had arrived in *wagons-lits*. On their luggage they had labels reading *Bad Theresienstadt*. Their luggage had been carried to their compartments by Waffen-SS officers. *"Auf Wiedersehen."* Now they were like fish floating on the surface of a remote pool in the company of other colourful fish, all of them belly up. They were sitting on a chair that stood up only because it leaned against a wall.

Leah knew an elderly man who had been a professor of astronomy at Heidelberg. He had researched the probability of life on distant planets. Among the women she knew was one Rosalie Ganzi, who told fortunes using playing cards. Rosalie had brought with her from Copenhagen photos of all her lovers. She would gaze at them with glassy eyes.

"They lured a lot of them here," Leah said, slowly, "people who'd won kudos for Germany. They promised them spa treatments and privileges. I can imagine what the German language meant to them; it was the language they spoke. They were promised they wouldn't be moved anywhere else. Instead, we'll all be going. We'll be sent to Poland, all of us."

"My God," Vili said. "A little more optimism wouldn't hurt you."

She moved into the light, like a light herself. I didn't want to think of her as someone who'd sold herself. (If push came to shove, wouldn't I sell myself too? The whole world was for sale, even the most honest people.)

"Did you set out the cards?" Vili asked. He looked at the packing crate on which some tarot cards were scattered.

"The worst ones came up for me," she answered.

"You're always exaggerating," he said.

"Is killing a person like killing the whole world? Is saving a person like saving the whole world? I wish I knew." Then she went on: "I'd like to be kind to the old people next door. I hate what's happening to them."

She looked out of the dormer window. "Been raining since this morning. The right cards didn't come up for me. It's my nerves. Don't tell me I'm hysterical."

Vili was tall and slim. The heavy work was doing him good, as it did me. By Leah's side he showed no outward traces of injury, want or worries due to the railway construction. He now had deeper lines above the bridge of his nose and at the corners of his mouth, sharper features, a high forehead. His elongated skull, his ruffled chestnut hair, beginning to grey at the temples. Less hair than before.

I could sense Leah's presence even though I was not looking at her. It was like swimming underwater and trying to touch one another. I was being drawn down by an irresistible current or vortex. An untouchable magnet was drawing me to her. Ebb and flow. I felt close to her. It had happened quickly – as it does for people who haven't got much time. If I bet on Vili not having noticed, I'd probably lose. It was he who'd taught me back in Prague never to underestimate anyone. She said "Yes" a few times, and each time it sounded different.

"It's pleasanter to look at a pretty face than not." He was slowly undressing and dressing again.

"You're lucky," I said.

"Maybe." Was there a note of pride?

Two long bedbugs were crawling across the ceiling. On the walls were dark blotches, the squashed drops of blood. The partitions were of pressed straw bound with cement; the one of undressed brick was darker. The door didn't close properly. The room was bound to be damp even in summer. It was inadequate insulation. In my mind I was calling her to me.

"I prefer the sun," she said. "I used to spend my summers

with my grandmother on a small estate with a pond and a quarry. I'd sit in a crack in the rock. In the evening I'd run up to the rock to say goodnight to the sun, and in the morning I said good morning to it. I was jealous of other children who also liked the sun. I wanted to have a privileged position. I was an only child, I was forgiven everything. When there's not much sun, I'm subject to the ugliest moods."

I made some remark about sunflowers.

"I can't guarantee your weather," Vili said. "That's something even the Germans can't control."

The old people next door were quarrelling. One of them told another to go find another hotel if he didn't like it here. No-one here was at his beck and call like a servant. The same voice complained that they were like lice crawling over each other. One was accusing another of pissing himself even in daytime.

"I feel as if I'm in a bad hotel on the moon," she said. "I see them without hair, without teeth, hungry and neglected, trapped in lethargy, guilty without guilt, beaten up even without wounds. They can't sleep. Sometimes they can't hold it when they're going to the latrine. What would I do in their place?"

She stepped up to the wall of unrendered brick and squashed a bedbug. She wiped her thumb on a rag by the window.

"It was dead already," she said.

"Pity you can't say that of its brothers," Vili remarked. "Where do they keep coming from?"

"Ugh," she said. She inspected her thumb. Something about her confused me. The waistcoat was lying on the bed, dry by now. Which was more than could be said of Vili's things or mine. Was she trying to kill time until they dried? She closed her eyes and half opened her lips. Was I crediting her with qualities she didn't have? I wanted to tell her how pretty she was, but I was trying hard to appear reserved. I avoided any flattery that might make Vili suspicious.

I pictured Leah in Leeuwarden in a house where everybody had their dressing gowns, where they changed the eiderdown covers, sheets and pillowcases every day. Where everyone could have everything instantly. Leah, meanwhile, was mopping up the puddles we'd made with a piece of sacking.

From next door came the continuation of an old quarrel or perhaps a new one, followed by an awkward silence. It highlighted the advantages that Vili and Leah enjoyed in their attic. (Agreeable qualities become more pronounced in the presence of something disagreeable.)

"It's cold in here," she said. "I'm sorry. We've nothing to use for heating."

"It's not too bad," I said.

"And it's damp."

"It's damp everywhere."

"The one thing those old folk can still do is make a noise," she said. "The noise proves they're still alive."

"That makes sense," Vili said. "Maybe they don't even hear it."

"They're alone."

"Sooner or later we'll all be."

"I wouldn't like to be alone."

"You're not."

"They can't sleep. One old woman next door has got stomach ulcers. Another has diarrhoea. Has to go to the latrine, into the rain, into the cold."

"Who'd want to get used to things here?"

"I would," I said.

"You've got a fortunate temperament."

Did Vili believe I wanted to get used to conditions here?

Didn't everybody have diarrhoea?

I looked at their books on the shelf, more from embarrassment than interest.

"Would you like to borrow something to read?" she asked.

"Some other time . . ." I managed. It would be an opportunity to come again, perhaps when Vili was out.

"Henry Miller," she said, pointing to one of the spines. "He lived a long time in Paris. He wrote more openly than others of his generation."

"Didn't have a special style for writing," Vili said. "Wrote straight from the shoulder. He wasn't admitted into polite society."

"I'd probably admit him."

"Your tolerance knows no limits," Vili said.

"Nor my sincerity." I could hear sarcasm in her voice.

An earwig walked across the spine of a book, but she didn't bother to kill it. I killed it myself. I squashed the bug with the tip of my finger. There was a clicking sound.

"Who knows what authors will write about us," Vili said. "I'd suggest to them the story of a captivating beauty who ages faster than is actually possible. About her friends, brides who didn't manage to marry soon enough, and about suitors who couldn't marry at all, and not only because they didn't want to commit." There was also sarcasm in Vili's words.

I could guess what Leah despised. She showed me a little volume, a paperback, tattered and dog-eared – Hemingway's

The Sun Also Rises – and said: "Lost souls. Or so they thought. They had nothing to compare themselves to then."

"It's always like that. Things in relation to other things," Vili said. "Freud and Marx knew what they were talking about. Everything develops and everything is connected with everything else." Then he said: "I'm a person who doesn't admit to debts, unless I have to." He looked at me. I blushed again.

It reminded me of little Ruth Winternitz.

"I'm quite curious to know how our life here will inspire future writers," Vili continued.

"Do things really change? Am I different every day?"

"Except in the ways you remain the same. In what everyone has from his mother and grandmother."

"I've got John Gunther's *Inside Europe* and *Inside Asia*. Very instructive even though things have changed since he wrote them. They're about the prominent figures of his day: Greta Garbo, Charlie Chaplin, Theodore Roosevelt and that painter from Vitebsk, Marc Chagall, who lived in Paris. Who knows what happened to him? He painted lovers before they became rabbis or cantors, long after they stopped singing because love was all they needed. A time when people lived joyously."

"I don't think it's ever too late," Vili added.

"I'm inviting you for New Year's Eve," Leah said, suddenly changing the subject. "We celebrated the last one *à deux*; we can celebrate the next one *à trois*."

Then she said: "This morning the old people hung black rags from their door and window to let the self-management people know there was a body to remove. They'll be needing a lot of black rags. While you were out, the Block Elder brought along a questionnaire from the management. They had the gall to ask for more statistics to submit to the Commandant's office. How are those old folk meant to complete it?"

"I don't give a damn about any of them," Vili declared. "The only one who isn't a villain is Gottlieb Faber," he added.

We hung up our things on the second beam under the roof. Again I noticed the bruises on Leah's arms and the pinch marks on her calves. How inaccessible was she? How available? Was I picturing Leah from Leeuwarden naked, in the attic of the old people's home, and then again dressed but without underwear? Without Vili Feld? It was possible to do this in my mind.

"Age strips people of shame," she said. "Of the strength to be ashamed. I don't like it when my skin peels, when my hair gets wiry and when my face is like emery paper."

She seemed as smooth as porcelain to me.

I sensed tension between them.

I wanted to know more about her. A moment later I realized I wanted to know everything about her.

"I feel like a fading flower," she said. "I think my life is madness. Once I regarded anything I didn't understand as ludicrous, later it frightened me, now it's all the same to me. I hadn't thought that even here people would envy one another, be jealous of one another and inflict – if not the worst – on each other, then rarely anything good."

"What did you expect? That they would wipe our bottoms for us?"

"I'll have to read the Bible more." She disregarded Vili's outburst. "Can a person be mad and at the same time realize she's mad?"

Vili looked at her. Was that his way of reprimanding or of reminding her?

Was she measuring her touch of madness by means of her sane intellect? It was obvious that her nerves were frayed. I could see it in her eyes. But at the same time she was smiling.

I had rarely been on my own, and when I had it hadn't bothered me. I knew it wouldn't be for long. Did being alone revive in her some disease people had no name for yet? It was invisible, like pain. What madness was she talking about?

"Whenever you're away, I imagine that my father will be shot after the war. It even makes me forget the stables where old horses were better off than people are here."

I pricked up my ears. She was bringing up a father Vili presumably knew about.

"I wouldn't think about that needlessly if I were you," he said.

Then she added (possibly for my benefit): "When I was a little girl, my father gave me a pearl. I gave it to a beggar. So he could sell it and buy some bread and shoes for himself. My father was very angry. That was the same day he told my mother to decide whether she preferred God or him. He didn't come home that night. He told my mother she could stuff her religious ideals."

"I've been told how pearls are born," Vili said. "The oyster defends itself against a parasite by secreting mother-of-pearl to encase it. From ugliness and sickness it produces a pearl. Humans aren't so lucky. Fortunately, there is more than one kind of beauty."

Leah didn't say anything more about her father. What would he be shot for after the war? She hinted that her mother had been deeply offended by her father and had taken that affront with her, via Westerborg, to Terezín and then to Poland. Leah had been on her own in the fortress for over a year. What had she learned? To blaspheme. To say what she thought.

About the old people next door Leah remarked: "I can no longer tell which are men and which are women. They look and sound the same."

Vili almost cut her off. "You observe them too closely."

"What else can I do? They're always there in front of me."

"You don't need to worry about them," Vili said. "They don't worry about you."

Leah turned to me. "When a woman ages, men no longer admire her. Most of those old folk had children. Where are they?"

"You aren't ageing any more than anybody else," Vili said. "I know people who'd be happy to age inside your skin."

(I'm one, I said to myself, shamelessly.)

"In your place I wouldn't give a damn."

Leah squashed another bedbug. She pressed the ball of her finger on the bedbug's back like a seal. She dipped her fingers in the washbasin that had been collecting rainwater, wiped them on her skirt. She bent down and I was alarmed as her skirt rode up. She showed a little of her thighs. Then she said: "They were as close to God as He is far from them now."

Across the road the roofs were shiny with rain. The chimneys looked like boots in puddles. The old people were fighting – in German – about a candle someone had stolen. One could tell from their accents what part of Germany they'd come from. (During the night one of them would be killed on the stairs on their way to the latrine. "*Erledigt*, finished," someone shouted in a croaky voice. "*Erledigt*.")

"They are like mice," Leah said. "The worst of it is that I'm rushing headlong in their direction."

"For heaven's sake, stop rushing. Slow down. Or do I have to quote Shakespeare to you – that all the world's a stage and all the men and women merely players, they have their exits and their entrances? You don't have to make your past into a crutch."

There were more old people than there was accommodation for them, even though more transports were leaving for the East. New people were arriving all the time. Twice already, transports had left with old and incurably sick people, including mental cases from the Kavalier barracks. New people kept arriving from Germany, Holland and Austria, as well as from Bohemia and Moravia. The Germans were doing everything possible for *Entjudung*.

"I'm not worried that I might be old like them."

The fading light touched Leah like a secret idea. Vili looked at her as one might look at a spoiled child.

"Have we got enough water for tea?" he asked.

"Enough for you to drown in tea," she replied.

She was listening to the rain falling into the dormer window, on the gutter and on the roof tiles.

"How about bread and margarine?"

"I've got something better."

"What could be better than margarine?"

"Ersatz. Artificial honey made from coal. Germany's triumph over nature. I'd love to offer you something even nicer. That'll have to wait until we're wonderfully off. At the moment we're only well off."

I didn't want them to quarrel. They were no longer smiling so much. Once again I noticed the bruises on her arm.

On a packing case she put a gadget with some whitish paraffin cubes and hung a kettle above it. She sliced some bread. (Where did she get her bruises?)

"I wouldn't drive a dog out into this."

She knew I'd have to stay. She mentioned that she had been splitting mica and that her eyes, her back and her behind had hurt, but she'd got out of it thanks to an acquaintance Vili had in the Central Registry, Gottlieb Faber. I wondered, both then and later, what she'd done in return.

"I praised the baker in the Sudeten barracks too much. Now he sells flour as if it was gold dust."

"You mustn't praise these people," Vili said. "Otherwise you'll pay three times as much next time."

"He's doing awfully well here. Is he hoping the war won't ever end? He's better off than before. He's become a predator just like the Nazis. Without being aware of it, the Germans have made Nazis of a lot of people. The only difference is their nationality. They don't wear uniforms. Often they don't even speak German. He seized his chance. Like my father. People from the *Transportleitung* choose whatever they please from the suitcases left behind. The baker has no other aim than feathering his own nest. He's getting fat and dresses like a count. Maybe he even prays. He can't imagine that you'd do any differently in his place. We all have the strength to steal. We fight with one another just like those old people next door. Where does the baker get his flour? He wouldn't care if 99 out of a hundred died of starvation. Why am I upset about it? Because I need him."

"Nobody kills the goose that lays the golden egg," I said.

"There are quite a few such people here."

"Aren't you rather too severe with yourself?" Vili asked Leah.

"People shouldn't do what he does," Leah said, still about the baker. "It's shameful."

For a few people the war was a gold mine. This did not include the old, the infirm, children or the adamantly honest ones who clung to their good names as the last remnant of what they'd brought with them, stubbornly and desperately, like drowning men clutching at straws. I didn't pity any of those greedy people when they were put on a transport. Those who hadn't managed to fix it so that someone else went in their place, someone like myself, Leah's mother, my friend Adler or, earlier, Ruth Winternitz.

Leah had sold the baker a portable gramophone with a set of Caruso records left to her by her father. Before that, Caruso's voice had rung through the small attic singing arias by Donizetti, Bizet and Verdi.

In the old people's room they were pushing furniture and palliasses about. Someone asked – without getting an answer – what the use was of a table without chairs. Judging by their panting, the task was beyond them. They knocked into something, something fell down. The wall shook. Was someone pressing his ear to it to listen to what we were saying?

We felt the warmth of the flames. Why was Leah worrying about ageing at 18? There was a veiled quality to her voice. She spread the artificial honey on the bread. With a knife in her hand she didn't look so frail.

"I remember a story of goldfish from school – they have short memories. Once round the bowl and they've forgotten where they came from."

She smiled. She was somewhere else now, fortunately. Vili couldn't have had an easy time with her. I tried to guess how long it would take for my things to dry.

We sat down to eat.

"I'm hungry as a wolf," Vili said to me.

He didn't let the noise of the old people disturb him.

"Mr Cohen is losing his memory. He no longer remembers the names of the stars. He babbles to himself: Acamar, Menkalinan, Kornephoros. I feel sorry for him."

"He's also losing control of his bowels," Vili said. "Spends hours sitting on the latrine."

"He has a cold and a soar throat," she admitted.

"He wears two of everything."

"They feel the cold," she said.

"He's not the only one."

Leah saw me looking at the pot of cosmetic cream made from margarine or fat. Mercury to erase freckles? Considering where we were this seemed excessive. (I had seen girls making themselves up on the stairs, in the yard or in some corner, using a window for a mirror, girls who combed their hair in the street and rouged their cheeks with brick dust. I was surprised women in the ghetto found the time and the will to do this; most of them would have to make do with plain water. Some still had a lipstick or some peroxide from before.) New transports kept arriving. To know somebody in the *Transportleitung* was a piece of luck. (Later, in Poland, the women looked different, their hair cut and shaved, on their heads and down below.)

We indulged in our artificial-honey sandwiches.

"In July a girlfriend of mine from Leeuwarden was selling perfume. During the day she worked in a tent in the square, attaching spare parts to engines, then she worked in the mica shop, and in the evenings she made a little extra money. She married a man a good deal older than herself. She wore make-up to the end. Even put some on when she went away on a transport."

"We want to look our best for the journey," Vili declared.

I ate. My palms were still painful from carrying the buckets. Sitting next to Leah, I held on to something that hovered behind our glances. A little while earlier we hadn't known one another. There had been a challenge and a longing in her voice, and I had tuned in to them. Or was it just a question of desire, and was I kidding myself? I hoped she might be able to read my thoughts, the ones that escaped Vili. To let my "yes" connect with her "yes".

"Feeding the body is not enough," she said.

"The Neanderthals believed that the body perishes but the soul lives on, trying to chase its imagined immortality."

"Are you being cynical? The body means such a lot to you?"

They had a shelf half covered with a curtain of blue velvet. Nothing much, but more than the old people next door had, or myself with Adler. Leah followed my glance.

"My father had his shirts, suits and shoes made to measure. He ordered my clothes from the same tailor. Maybe I'll wear some of them yet."

She enjoyed serving food to us. She was both very much a girl and very much a woman. This blurred the age gap between her and Vili. I'd suit her much better, I thought. She kept half smiling. She had small white teeth. Her movements were slow. She reached with one hand for the plates, a dishcloth over the other arm. One plate, another, then the third. The box on which she'd set out her tarot cards served as our table. The skin on her arms and shoulders was smooth, and on her nape, below her hair, she had fine golden down.

I began to understand where she and Vili had come from and what they were trying to remind themselves of. Eating had made me happy. If I'd been able to, I'd have eaten, chewed, swallowed and sung or bawled at one and the same time.

She had observed my animality without saying anything. I sensed her participating in it.

"That was excellent," Vili said.

"I hope so," she answered. "You need to be a magician here."

Her choice of words – we were all speaking German – was elegant. She shaped them slowly on her lips. For a moment I had the impression that she was making an effort for me.

"The worst light here is 60 days before and after the shortest day," she said.

The rain was drumming on the roof. The thunder had stopped. A little later I learned why she'd said that she imagined her father being shot after the war. She came from a family in which there was no love lost. Including the grandmother from Leeuwarden, from whom Leah had inherited the little attic room (with the help of Gottlieb Faber from the Central Registry), and her mother, who, for a few years, was the butterfly of social evenings in Leeuwarden but did not have a single woman friend who'd visit her. In Leeuwarden, Leah's father had collaborated with the Gestapo. He had been a vet who had treated race-horses. The Nazis had summoned him, originally, because of problems at the racecourse. He'd known the woman owner of the stables. She had refused to send her two-year-olds to Berlin. The Gestapo wanted information about punters. In the end the punters melted away. Leah's father sold each name for 150 marks, ten for 1,500. From the time she was a small girl she'd heard him talk about horses. He knew the backgrounds of the riders, the owners and the backers. She knew that a lot of money rode on the success or failure of the jockeys, horses and owners, as well as a lot of love, ambition and wrecked careers, and of detected and undetected fraud. (Even then, she might have asked what human life was worth.) Not to mention people who'd shot themselves in the head, drowned themselves in alcohol, or got lost without a trace.

At 13, Leah had become involved with a jockey who came just about up to her chest. She'd had an affair with a tenor who was 37 years her senior – until he developed a preference for the Berlin opera. (He'd claimed that Hitler in his youth had composed an opera and that Jewish theatre managers had turned it down.) When her parents were out, Leah would invite the tenor round: he'd sing arias from Wagner's operas to her and cracked her father's bowl of Czech ruby glass.

"Fathers", she said, "don't forgive their daughters' sins, never mind how many they've committed themselves. Why does every father want his daughter to be better than himself?"

"Sons are probably different."

"I had a fine specimen of a father," she said. "Who knows where he is now?"

She recalled their conversation before he'd been put on the transport. She'd accused him of having sold his soul. He asked what that was. Could one hold it in one's hand? Swallow it? Was the soul in one's chest? In one's teeth? Or in one's heart, one's blood, or one's shadow? Was it an adornment like earrings worn by women or sailors? No-one had ever seen a soul. I tried to imagine her father when he told her he'd be glad if things were that simple.

He'd told her about a jockey who'd won all the Derbys for

his owner. One day the jockey discovered that his horse was blind. He trained him, groomed and fed him, and slept in his stable box. The blind horse won another great race for a big prize. At the next race he crashed into a barrier and killed the jockey and himself. It was lucky, her father told her, that he didn't kill more people.

"No-one likes having a father who is a criminal."

Leah had been looking after her grandmother from Leeuwarden. She didn't want anyone else to get the attic. The grandmother had dragged her 90 years to Terezín like a sack into which she'd stuffed everything. She used to speak German to Leah, even though she'd lived in Leeuwarden for 73 years. Hers had been an arranged marriage. She'd been born into an Orthodox family, and she was Orthodox herself. Physical contact was distasteful to her. Semen disgusted her. Grandfather had a mistress who lived with them. Leah's grandmother had looked after five children. Life from the waist down was a duty for her. She produced Jewish children. She never touched anything, she never learned anything.

After their arrival, Leah had been housed in the Girls' Home on L 418. On her sixteenth birthday, the schoolmistress had caught her in the attic with her lover. They were chased out into the courtyard. They didn't have time to dress. They were made to face a court of honour. Leah was put down for the next transport to the East. Her defence was that she didn't want to miss anything. They asked her if she wasn't ashamed of herself. She said she felt she was an adult. A month later, the schoolmistress was surprised to find she hadn't left yet. That had been arranged by Gottlieb Faber, Vili's card-game partner.

For Leah and Vili, Gottlieb Faber was the finger of fate. I

could guess, later, what payment he exacted for his services. And what Vili closed his eyes to. As his rabbi grandfather had told him, Abraham had done the same with his own wife. For fear that Pharaoh would kill him, he declared her to be his sister, and he knew very well what Pharaoh was up to with her. (Vili also told me about King David, who slept with both women and men. It's in the Bible.) Leah knew that some unknown old man, sick mother or child would have to leave in her place. Everyone who remained here was living at the expense of somebody else, just as later on, anybody still alive was so because somebody else had been killed instead. When it is a matter of life or death, a person will find ways to excuse anything. (Literally.) This doesn't mean his conscience won't prick him. These pricks are invisible and sometimes painless. The self-preservation drive is like hunger or the urge to propagate. Something other than culture. This time one schoolmistress presided over the court of honour, a second acted as assessor, and girls were picked for the jury – in the same courtyard where Leah had been made to stand naked when she'd been caught with her lover. She spent several nights with Gottlieb Faber. Then she got a paper with the rubber stamp of the Council of Elders, and the attic was hers. (Faber told Leah she'd be wasted on any man who'd want her for himself alone. He didn't believe that friendship between men and women was possible. He'd keep her as long as she went along with the arrangement. After they parted he remembered her as a mirage.)

My clothes were drying. She was keeping me alive with a promise, enveloping me in a waking dream.

Down in the courtyard Leah and Vili had a shower made from a horse trough. (The fitters from the railway construction had helped them construct it.) The rainwater was icy, it didn't rinse the soap off well, and in summer there wasn't enough rain. Sometimes what came out of it was dirty slush. But it was more than the old people had, locked out as they were from the shower by a padlock on the door.

"Sometimes some of our food gets lost," Vili said. "Except that it doesn't."

Did she give some of it to the old people when he wasn't at home? (I later discovered that she'd done this a few times.)

"This morning a couple poisoned themselves. They were holding hands."

"Were they lovers?"

The sounds of her voice mingled with the dripping of the rain, with the fading light from the dormer window and the noises from next door.

She looked at Vili. (For a second, or two or five.) Did she believe that attractive people were meant to be with attractive people? She accepted that no-one was responsible for their birth. One dealt with most people according to their appearances. The Nazis had made this more prevalent. Why had that couple killed themselves? Were they frightened by their increasing weakness? Of the journey to the East? Of humiliation? Of a life for which no-one had prepared them and which they no longer had the strength to resist? It was easy enough to get hold of poison. They'd realized that it was easier to die than to live.

"In my next life I want to learn Czech," she said. "When I was a little girl I hoped the man I married would believe he'd chosen the best girl on the block."

She had overturned my first impression with a second one,

and the second with a third. We could hear the old people again.

"Fortunately, there's more than one kind of beauty." Vili spoke again.

I said I'd have to leave. She looked at me as if this was the last moment of her life. It occurred to me that she was given to exaggerating. The way she envisaged her father being hanged if he survived the war and returned from the East. Did she see herself ageing? Wrinkle by wrinkle? She had bruises and circles under her eyes, yet a porcelain complexion. I was waiting for Vili to unpack the waistcoat. Our clothes should be dry by now. Did they still need me for something, perhaps to be a witness? I could hear the old people going to the latrine. Someone fell on the stairs. Or crashed into the wall.

"Rivers flowing into a sea that's no longer there."

"What about Faber?" Vili asked.

"He doesn't want love, or even beauty, maybe just freshness. That's more important to him than any woman."

In the corner of the attic was a mouse hole.

At one time the German university at Heidelberg had refused to admit Gottlieb Faber. Later he became a university professor. Before coming to the fortress, he'd swept the floors in the textile mill he owned. He had a talent for mathematics and an excellent memory. The gamblers in Heidelberg hadn't denounced him only because he didn't cheat. He'd managed to keep his family by playing cards just one night a month. The police in Bucharest advised him to move to another country. The police in Berlin ordered him to emigrate. Unfortunately, he went to Holland, occupied by the *Wehrmacht* in a blitzkrieg move. Gottlieb Faber was once more on German soil. He knew Dutch by then. He had come to Terezín via Westerborg.

Vili began to unpack the waistcoat, a small warehouse of necessary and useful little things. I saw that he knew what was important. I felt as though I was visiting a nouveau riche. He laid out small bags of sugar, flour, semolina, lentils and peas on the bed. For a moment, Leah's mind seemed to be elsewhere. Had she forgotten what she had said? (It was ridiculous to talk about beauty or ageing in the fortress. Everybody was in danger of being transported to the East, the old people of dying before their turn came.)

Vili was like a hunter with his booty. He gave Leah a pair of woollen socks, a scarf and some fur-lined slippers. And a bundle of 20-mark notes in a rubber band.

"Thanks. I still like it if something belongs only to me."

"It's a different kind of pleasure," Vili agreed.

What about my cigarettes?

"You know why I'm nervous. I don't want to keep Faber waiting."

"There'll be something here for Faber as well. You can take it to him. That should be sufficient."

"You know very well that it won't be enough for him. It wouldn't be enough for me either."

I wondered what kind of arrangement Vili had with Faber. Or did Faber have an arrangement with Leah? I didn't like seeing somebody sharing or selling the woman he was living with. Or letting him have her, say, once or three times a week. I was progressing from one surprise to another. Again I realized how pretty she was. Was this a part, or even the whole basis, of their existence here? Who wouldn't wish to make the most of what they had? (I kept repeating this to myself.) I probably blushed again. Hadn't I – though perhaps differently – served Vili Feld and, indirectly, those two women in the maize field? And, directly, Leah from Leeuwarden?

"While he was waiting for you yesterday," she said, "he made fun of the so-called codes of honour – truthfulness, respectability, honesty. It pays, he said, to turn them upside down. Cheat, lie, deceive. To tell the truth is ridiculous. To appeal to one's conscience in a conflict? That's a sock with holes in it. You either darn it or throw it away. You won't get far otherwise. Keep your word? Don't even think of it. Maybe not even to yourself, he said. Guilt? Let somebody show him someone who's free from guilt."

"Don't take him literally."

"He knows what he's talking about."

"Only with you."

"You think I'm that naive?" she asked.

"I didn't say so."

"I did."

She was beautiful under the shadow of anger that veiled her eyes. She smoothed her hair. I noticed a few spots on her white linen skirt. Even anger did not make her unattractive.

"I'll soon go grey what with him and with you."

I looked at the things on the bed.

"I said to Faber that even an older man can look worn down and still feel young. I won't list the reasons why this doesn't apply to women. He reprimanded me for having felt old even at 13. I know when Faber is lying to me. Why he's treating me like a ten-year-old. Does he want me to think he can do anything? He recommended platonic love to me if I didn't want to suffer."

"He probably knows what he's talking about."

Leah kept silent.

"Beauty is death," she then said.

"Don't exaggerate."

"A flower growing in the Arctic."

"Thank you for the meal," I said.

"Have you dried out?"

"Better than I expected."

"Next time I'll lend you an umbrella." She smiled.

Leah was looking at me with the expression of a person who doesn't wish to be thanked. (She did this again later, in different circumstances.) Vili was rearranging the items from the waistcoat. He appreciated what the two women had brought him. Suddenly I was on his side. We had smuggled those things together, sharing the risk. For the same woman. How and whom was she prepared to serve?

She moved very close to him. As Vili picked each item up and put it down again, I felt Leah and I were losing contact. The little bags shone in the half-light. They took up the entire bed. I couldn't interpret the misty expression on Leah's face. I could see what those things meant to her. (What they'd mean to anybody here.) In the fortress, where people sold themselves out of hunger, they dreamed day and night of eating their fill. Of having something for their child, their old mother, a sick friend. Something for the evening, the night and tomorrow. Being satiated was morality, hunger was immorality. I thought of the wives who were unfaithful with their husband's silent consent, I thought of daughters who managed to obtain something extra for their fathers or mothers in the only way open to them. Of a body given in exchange for medication, for an aspirin, for thin, bluish milk.

"In a wolf pack, the females prefer the older and more experienced males. But they want to have their cubs by a young wolf. On the other hand, the males – of any age – want the strongest females," Vili said.

"What makes you say this?"

"Beauty and lies are not mutually exclusive."

"Either something's the truth or it isn't beautiful."

"Sometimes beauty is a lie. We all know when a lie is beautiful."

"I don't know what you mean."

"No-one is flawlessly beautiful," he said evasively. "Sometimes the flaws just can't be seen."

The old glint was in his eyes, just as there was infinity or a refusal to yield in Leah's. Experience and perhaps wisdom. Cleverness, a bit of selfishness, an ability or promise to share. Did this apply to both of them? Everything was suddenly as it had always been between Vili and me, except that I'd grown up. What was there left for me to find out about them? I was waiting for my share from the waistcoat.

"You always beat me."

That was what I called his glint. The invisible magic without and within. The flash in his glance that contained a dozen other qualities.

He turned to me. "I'm thinking of my mother. She was beautiful, in a different way from Leah. I often dream of her."

I tried to understand what it meant for him to have survived instead of his older brother.

"I saw a photograph of my mother," I said.

We were looking at the things on the bed.

He turned to Leah. "I don't want you to think that you're

ageing every second. Things are better for us than for thousands of others."

"I don't want to think about it," she said. "I'm no longer thinking about it."

"It's a waste of energy."

The shutters squeaked. Leah was holding the scarf and other things in her arms like a child. Uneven beams of light were moving over her hair.

"No letter today?"

"I haven't been through everything yet," Vili replied.

In my mind I compared Leah with the photograph of my mother. I hadn't thought about my mother for some time. I thought about my unknown father. I wondered what my mother had looked like when she was 18 and I was already on the way. Those first 35 days when my sex was still undecided. Was my ability to see in the dark a feminine characteristic? Or the way I tried to get what I desired? What would I have to know to understand my unknown father?

Vili picked up the waistcoat again. He examined the pockets. He felt the padded shoulders, the hems and the seams. Was he looking for a letter? Nothing rustled. The last thing he extracted from the toughest part of the waistcoat was a bag hidden between pieces of cardboard in the shoulder padding.

"What is it?" Leah wanted to know.

It was a flat 35-calibre automatic pistol. Leah shut her eyes. Vili wordlessly slipped the pistol into the pocket of his dressing gown. My heart started hammering again. The wind was blowing raindrops into the room through the dormer. The clouds were low; in a while, when I left, the darkness would touch them.

"At the beginning of the war, I met my Communist cousin at the Mousehole in Jungmannovo náměstí. We hadn't seen each other for nine years. He pulled out some leaflets and wanted me to distribute them. I vanished as fast as I could, hoping I wouldn't see him again for another nine years at least."

Would I try to escape if I had a gun? Would I be able, say from an ambush, to shoot down the worst people in the Commandant's office, like Karl Rahm, the Commandant, or Heindl? Or Anton Burger? Or their mistress on her white horse, the blonde telephonist? Or some of my own people, the vilest, the most ruthless or the most disagreeable? Or Gottlieb Faber if he picked my index card and, instead of his chance mistress, assigned me to the next transport? Only after a while did the idea of a pistol give rise to the idea of suicide. That was something close to everyone. Everyone felt they were on the borderline. Between what had been and what would never be again. For the moment one just needed to survive. But a gun meant more. What had the two women in the maize field expected of Vili, the women who by now were (hopefully) safe? When would they make another trip? Would I be content with killing the vice-chairman of the Council of Elders, the rabbi with the Hungarian wife whom he alternated with young girls? Girls whom he exempted from transport at someone else's expense? Or Dr Friedmann, who saved a wagonload of flour each month from our already inadequate rations? I despised them as the Germans despised us. Was I hoping, like that baker from Leeuwarden who sold his bread and flour to Leah, that the war would go on because he'd never made so much money before? The pistol had turned me into a judge – also of myself.

"Is it loaded?" I asked.

"Probably not."

I imagined that it was my pistol. Who would dare face me if I had a pistol with the requisite number of bullets? How, I wondered, would the Commandant or his blonde, whom he shared with Anton Burger and whose horse was looked after by a Jewish coachman, behave if I were lying in wait as they walked home to tell their German children the story of Hänsel and Gretel? My head was spinning. How they all would beg, tremble and cry. I have to do it, I'd say. Vengeance and justice intertwined in me like dusk and night.

"I see things in black and white. Don't you?"

Vili took his time to reply. The pistol had caught him unawares. I was wondering what was important to him. Did I at that moment wish that he had a bolder heart? Was I pleased that he was afraid?

"Somebody ought to calculate how many people lost their lives through carelessness or through the actions of their comrades," Vili said.

"The sergeant would have loved that pistol," I remarked.

A shiver ran down my spine. His too, probably.

Leah was watching us.

There was in his voice the tone of someone caught out doing something they didn't want to be caught out at. I recalled the gaze of the two women who had brought the waistcoat. There was a draught from the window. I'd have to go out into the rain. Leah was looking at me. There was eagerness in her eyes. Excitement at the unexpected.

"Who are you talking about?"

"People who feel it's their duty to repay debts."

At the bottom of a parchment tub filled to the rim with

caramel were eight bullets, each separately wrapped. He slipped them into his other pocket.

"I'd kill if I had to, to stop them killing me," Leah said. "For what they've already done to us."

She didn't say what part her father had in all this. Would she perhaps kill him too?

"Are you playing Joan of Arc?" Vili asked.

"To be afraid has nothing to do with one's sense of responsibility."

"Maybe you should be afraid a little more."

"I'm more afraid than you think. For you and for myself."

"I'll be satisfied if you're careful." There was irritation in his voice. Suddenly what he'd brought seemed not very much. He looked at her. I could sense his displeasure.

"My aim is to stay alive," Vili said. "One day you'll live as you want to. Go where you wish. Do whatever you choose. Say what you think. To whomever you choose."

"How far into the corner do they have to push you?" Then she said: "I'd rather have things be clean. I don't want to live with a bad conscience. Dissemble. Deny who I am. It doesn't amuse me to do something I don't believe in. Like my father."

"I don't like you comparing me to him."

The presence of the pistol had changed us. There was something we hated within ourselves, maybe even more than we hated our enemies. It was like stripping naked, like having nothing to cover yourself with. In the officers' mess they were playing "Heidi". They played that record several times a day. Followed by military marches. The sounds dissolved in the drumming of the rain.

Vili turned to me. "Let me give you some advice. Don't live

with a hysterical woman. Or with a woman who doesn't want to grow old. Or one who wants the world to go round the way she wishes it to. Who doesn't acknowledge anything. It's difficult to say no to her, to put even a little feather in her path. Maybe she'd enjoy dying young and beautiful. Jumping over her shadow." He was angry and didn't hide it.

"Would you be able to kill?" Leah asked me.

Was she accusing him of cowardice? Had she not understood what he'd said to me because he'd spoken in Czech?

"If I had to," I echoed her.

"What will you do?" Leah asked Vili.

"Won't you at least admit that men have a tendency to think before they act?"

I thought of the German telephone operator and her lovers in the Commandant's office and I thought of the pistol. It all blurred in my mind. The sergeant. The Jewish general who surrendered the last fortress to the Romans, to whom – to this day – an ambiguity clung, something unforgivable if explicable, a shadow of doubt. We didn't yet know about the 23-year-old commander of the Warsaw Ghetto rising who, in the last bunker alongside his fighters who preferred to shoot themselves rather than fall into the hands of the Germans, killed first his mother and then – with his last bullet – himself. There weren't many who had a choice. And Vili didn't yet know that in Auschwitz-Birkenau he'd be made an assistant capo and block leader, that he'd walk round the camp with a stick, occasionally letting it descend on the backs or heads of undisciplined inmates, his fellow Jews (and slap the face of my friend Adler, because they knew each other from the Hagibor, to stop him pestering Vili with requests for bread). And that, after the war, he'd be just like Leah and wouldn't want to be what he was.

"A hundred cigarettes doesn't seem enough for so much trouble," Vili said. "Here's two hundred."

He turned to Leah. "Shall I equip your old woman with a pistol? Or arm all the old women, the infants, the young mothers and the sick? Encourage the men of military age to stage a rising with one pistol?"

"I am being ridiculous," Leah said.

Perhaps it had occurred to her that they were both right.

Vili gave me two hundred cigarettes and two bars of chocolate, a German and a Swiss one. Both had pretty coloured wrappings. As far as his keeping his word was concerned, I couldn't complain. Was it anything to do with a good or generous heart? With how the fortress turned people into better or worse characters? You could still buy things in Prague, if you had the money. The black market was flourishing everywhere. On the Swiss chocolate wrapper was a picture of a cow and a vat of white milk and three hazelnuts without their leaves; the German one showed a pilot with a gourmet's smile, wearing a leather jacket and standing by the wing of a fighter plane, snow-capped Alps in the background. I'd done better than I'd expected.

He put up the blanket again so I could change. Perhaps it only seemed that she slapped Vili's face and he hers? I didn't see anything, I only heard. Would this explain the bruises on her arms?

"I'm sorry," I heard.

"Why d'you do that?" she asked.

"I could ask you the same."

I reconciled myself to the fact that I wouldn't understand

anybody even if I lived a thousand years. She looked naked in her clothes. It all came down to physical presence. The thing that makes life so difficult for us compared to the animals. The thing that makes us poison nature despite the rabbis, who don't acknowledge happiness as happiness, pleasure as pleasure. But without which everything might be worthless. I was more confused than I'd been at the beginning.

Her voice had aged. I had lost them both now.

"You're off?" Vili asked. "I'll see you home."

"In a minute," I said.

"I'll go ahead. I'll wait downstairs."

I put on my boots.

I could tell he was fed up with her. I put on my damp cap, visor backwards, like a jockey. Leah stood at the window. I couldn't see her face in the glass for the streaming rain. Was she crying? Through the now open door came the noises from the old people's home.

Vili shut it behind him.

"At night it seems to me that the only question is when and how to defend yourself," she said into the darkness and the rain. "I blame myself for what my father did. I'd like to erase it. I know that can't be done. Maybe the ability to defend yourself is as important as breathing. I feel I am choking."

Was she saying this to me? Or to herself?

"I've got to mend my soul each day, just like a punctured tyre."

Leah from Leeuwarden turned, stepped over to me by the door. Without a word she embraced me as if I were someone she would never see again. I was waiting for her to say something, but she said nothing. I felt her body. This was not the desire to assert herself. There was haste and eagerness in her. Fear, anger and sympathy, rebellion. A wish to do something against what was diminishing her, humiliating her, making her fade. As if she were living her final second. Suddenly I had become a part of someone else's life, someone I hadn't known until that afternoon. (As had happened with the women in the maize field.) And just as quickly I was stepping out of it.

She looked fragile again, like someone dying second by second. She half opened her lips, bent towards me and kissed me – softly, moistly, with a touch of what people seek in each other and do not find, or what they find and simultaneously lose again. There was longing in her eyes. She smelled of tea and artificial honey. I had the impression she was kissing me and herself at the same time. She pressed her thighs against me. I felt her whole body for those few seconds. Both girlish and maternal. When she stepped away, she glanced at me, from my head over my crotch down to my feet and back. She dropped her eyes.

"Come round some time. I'll tell your fortune from the cards," she said.

"Thank you."

"Don't mention it."

She looked at me with her blue eyes as if through thick lace. In her voice was an echo of the resignation with which she shared herself with Gottlieb Faber and of her unwillingness which irritated Vili. I was seeking, beneath her skin, from close up, the tenderness she had in her voice when she wanted to, and for a split second I heard her ruthlessness – but maybe I wanted to hear it. For a second or two I was able to savour her company without anyone else being present. It seemed to me that there was a willingness to take risks in her glance. A promise and consent. Doubts. She looked like a flower that was losing its freshness but that was still beautiful. She had tired eyes.

"I don't want to keep Vili waiting," I said.

"I too – still – don't like to hurt other people." Then she added: "Unlike my father, I have not done anything wrong, and I've never betrayed anyone. Not even their expectations. I hate perfidiousness, but I've got used to it. I'm 18."

Under the roof of the former stables with the trough and the padlock on the door, Vili said: "No-one in the building is eating, and they all have diarrhoea. I don't know if anyone ever was or will be able to appreciate the advantages of youth."

Didn't it strike him that I'd been upstairs too long? Or didn't he care? Or had he wanted it?

"You don't live badly."

"I'm lucky sometimes."

"Evidently."

"It stinks here."

"You can't have everything."

"They empty it every eight months."

I looked at him.

"I dropped the pistol down the latrine," he explained.

I blushed.

"When your house is on fire, you're not going to wait for someone to tell you how to put it out. You can't gamble with the lives of others."

The blood was rising to my head.

"Isn't it true that opportunity makes a thief?" he asked. "Our small private war is a part of the big war."

"But isn't the big war also a war against you and me?" I asked. I didn't entirely understand him.

"That score will be settled by others when the time comes."

"In a war, as a rule, people use guns," I added.

"Last time there were anti-Nazi leaflets in the waistcoat."

"The Germans aren't yet at the point where they'll defeat themselves."

"We're all the Devil's allies. You don't help yourself by turning your back on him."

He could see that he wasn't convincing me. I felt as if he'd slapped my face. I'd already concluded that the women in the maize field had been there several times. Hadn't they had time to tell him what the waistcoat contained before I disturbed them? I had to admit that the better kind of person attached themselves to him. He surrounded himself with any beauty that was still accessible. Was he only interested in courage of a certain kind? A courage he found in those women? He'd reconciled himself to the fact that beauty and courage were both good and evil. To the fact that both were useful. The rest he gladly left to wiser men. And now, for the first time, he'd allowed me a glimpse of the good and evil aspects of beauty. I'd always regarded courage as a positive quality. The thought of defending myself excited me. I appreciated that when it came to women, he never ended up empty-handed. Among the better ones he'd probably find the best. Vili Feld, my former role model. The light that had attracted me. That glint in his eyes when I was 15. Ambition I was keen to copy. Experience I wanted to feed on. That invisible something at which he didn't even wish to be perfect.

"Our morals depend on our situations."

He looked tired just as Leah had.

"Her skin isn't as thick as she pretends it is when she squashes a bedbug with her thumb."

Then he remarked: "You can judge your importance by how you are seen by your lover, wife or companion, or even by your enemy. So long as you don't feel smaller than small or more worthless than worthless as a result."

And finally: "In her case you can't speak of exaggerated gratitude. Least of all of appreciation. She is more selfish than I thought."

I could see what he meant.

"I bet I know what she'll ask me when I get back."

I kept silent.

"Are we entitled to be cowards?"

I preferred not to say anything.

"Who hasn't got more than one morality? I myself have two or three. We only live once, as her father used to say. I don't envy rats; aren't they supposed to leave sinking ships first? Who'd wish to be the captain in such a situation?"

I felt like a boxer after a right hook to the chin and a left to the solar plexus. I had just enough time to rally. Not to fall to the floor.

And when I still remained silent: "You take things too seriously." As if he didn't.

Then he said: "The things a woman wants: solidarity, courage, control of her weaknesses, sympathy, inventiveness, tenacity, support – I could go on and on. As if it wasn't enough simply to cope and keep one's head above water. Sometimes you find yourself in situations where you can't win no matter what you do."

And finally: "I don't expect anyone will raise a monument to me. Nothing is for free. Not even sleeping with someone. Maybe that costs more than anything."

It later occurred to me that there are two sides to this argument. But that was a lot later.

I thought of when they would come from the sanitation department of the Council of Elders to empty the latrine. The Germans were afraid of epidemics. In Ravelin-2, the drained moat where the prisoners grew vegetables, they had two horse-drawn carts to carry waste, excrement and dirt into the fields. I remembered the waste pipes. (I was surprised the Commandant's office allowed the vegetables they ate to be fertilized with the excrement of the prisoners in the fortress. Somehow they must have overlooked that.) The latrine was hardly ever unoccupied. Twelve metres long, three metres wide, men and women separated by a screen; the pit was two and a half metres deep. I'd have to get a diver's suit from the Firemen's House. I'd hate to get shit all over me and then not find anything.

"A woman's decline begins when she identifies her worth with her beauty," Vili said. "Not with what is – still is – but with what no longer is. I don't know the cure for this. Evidently not the knowledge that everybody ages and we've got to learn to live with it."

There was something else on his mind. I was surprised at the confidences he was sharing with me. We'd had a rich afternoon.

I shifted my weight to the other foot.

He tried to lighten the atmosphere with one of his pre-war anecdotes. The pessimist believes that all women are whores.

The optimist hopes they are. As Nietzsche or Chekhov said: This is beyond good or evil. Beyond morality. For Dostoevsky beauty was sometimes the Devil and other times the saviour of the world. Everyone does what he can stand to do."

We both knew what he was trying to cover up.

Eventually he said: "A woman tells you she loves you. 'You're the best thing I've ever had in my life. My life is empty when you're not with me. I'm waiting for you – naked. Where are you? I miss you desperately. I want you madly. I love you to death.' A moment later, she does something practical. To protect herself. To have at least something of what the others have. A warm overcoat. Better underwear. Poppy-seed cakes instead of someone who pulls her out of a transport to the East."

I completed the picture in my mind. Why was he saying all this to me?

"She sleeps with you because she's afraid you might leave her."

What could he do with a person who saw death in her vanishing beauty? Something in her was connected to the pistol. I didn't know how. Later, in Auschwitz-Birkenau, when we were standing in front of Dr Mengele, it occurred to me that someone could have pushed the pistol into his mouth and squeezed the trigger. Many of those who no longer had any prospects would have been happy to do so. Those whose father, mother, daughter, son or friend had already been sent to the gas chamber, and they themselves to a labour squad. It wouldn't leave a stain on their consciences. They weren't really alive anyway. But this didn't happen – with the exception of the Jewish woman from Poland who'd brought a pistol into the underground undressing room, or snatched it from the man on duty, and shot him. One pistol wasn't much, but even a little was better than nothing.

"I don't like blood," Vili said. "I'm no hero. I wasn't born a killer, despite everything. I get goose pimples even thinking about it. Maybe one day I'll be one. But not yet. He who deals in blood perishes in blood."

In this respect I agreed with him.

I looked into the latrine. Old people were moving round us, men on one side and women on the other. They were dressed in rags, with worn-out shoes. They were shaking with fatigue; some came with umbrellas, with hats long out of fashion. There they sat, men and women, back to back, each on their side. They had hardly imagined the end of their lives would be like this.

"The Germans believe they were born to kill. They don't need a reason. Heroism and killing are one and the same thing to them. The one justifies the other."

It was still raining. We sheltered under the latrine's little roof. Thanks to the rain the stench was weaker now.

"I don't like massacres," Vili added. "Yesterday she invited the *Lausdoktor*. She can't bear dirt. Her beauty is like an egg she must hatch every day. The old people terrify her. She sees them in herself. But everyone is betrayed by their body. She is obsessed with physicality. She wants to be fond of everybody so everybody will be fond of her. When a woman gains strength through her beauty, she loses her strength."

He preferred talking about Leah from Leeuwarden to talking about the pistol in the latrine.

"That's what makes her happy or unhappy," he repeated. "That's all I can tell you about her."

I could imagine the rest. She couldn't bear solitude: she lost herself in it as though she didn't exist. Of the people she was with she expected the opposite of her father. She measured them by her father.

"That fine father of hers should have given her a snake's name. All she'd have to do is slough off her skin every spring, and she'd always look the same."

"Who wouldn't like that?"

"You're clever," he said.

"She's pretty."

"It's costing me enough."

"Is it meant to last?"

"So long as my strength and my nerves do."

"You seem to manage."

"You never know a person well enough, even if you live next to them or sleep with them. Nobody knows anybody. Is that good or bad? I don't know."

I recognized that voice. He was speaking to me as he'd done at the Hagibor. But this was different from the Café Aschermann, where I'd learned how to play poker elegantly from him. He'd had a set-to with the Aryan headwaiter at the Aschermann. He'd proved that the waiter had made a mistake in the bill, a mistake in the waiter's favour. In those days the law was on the headwaiter's side. If he'd let me choose whom I wanted for my teacher, I'd have chosen Vili.

He gave me his hand. I thought of Leah squashing bedbugs. As for the threesome we had accidentally become – the glint in Vili's eyes seemed to say – he hoped that our chance encounter had satisfied me. Perhaps not in every way. Who can have everything?

"You'll get wet again," he said.

"So what?"

"Let's hear from you some time."

"You will."

"We'll look forward to it."

I was struck by the "we". Did it include me the way it did Gottlieb Faber? The blood rose to my head. Into what category had he placed me? He asked if everything was all right. Had I got my cigarettes? I looked at him. We were almost the same height. And for the first time in years, I disliked something about him. It wasn't just the pistol he'd thrown away. He had no regrets.

I needed to divide the people with whom I had anything in common into good ones and bad ones, useful and useless ones. Outwardly I acted carefree, but inside I was in turmoil. I measured everybody by what Vili said, what he did, how he acted. I didn't recognize mitigating circumstances. I had to decide whom I would avoid in future. Hadn't Vili once told me that his father had carried two cards in his breast pocket? One had had the names of his friends, and the other, the names of those he didn't ever want to see again. Because his memory was beginning to go, he'd look at the two lists before shaking hands with anyone. Then he either stopped or walked on. I hadn't got to that point yet. But subconsciously I adopted the idea. I didn't have to write my lists down. Why waste time with someone, even if time was no longer as precious as it had been?

On my lips was the breath of Leah from Leeuwarden. A slight touch of guilt. It would evaporate in a moment. (I was mistaken in this.)

It was about 15 minutes to the water tower where Adler was working. I got on my way. Abruptly I turned. There was shouting from the latrine. I took a few steps into L Street. Past the stairs, and again I heard shouting from overhead. I didn't stop. But I walked more slowly. I hadn't a clue about their domestic wars or truces. About how they got on and how they didn't. Just as I had no clue about what beauty and time and dusk and light and wind, or spring and autumn, meant to Leah.

In my mind, I saw Vili's face with its clear-cut features, his narrow head and his thinning hair. He could no longer afford the light-heartedness of his life at the Hagibor which had allowed him to sleep well at night. Nevertheless he tried. That darker glint in his grey, wolfish eyes suggested a fatigue he didn't talk about. That dark starlight. Perhaps he had something else in his eyes as well – disappointment at what things had come to. His pure and false elegance. What had befallen a race that professed the word, the law and nobility and was vegetating now, in degradation, outside society, sentenced to a twilight between evening and night, pushed to the very edge where reason and right had no validity. Sunlight had turned into darkness, warmth into chill. Joy into sadness and nostalgia, song into lament. Perhaps he had an echo of his original magic in his eyes, of what he was suppressing in order to survive. Maybe even doubts that had not yet surfaced.

Hadn't he said, when, after the assassination of Heydrich, the threat of transport hung over Prague and the first people were leaving for Lodz – renamed Litzmannstadt after a German general – that this was the first hole torn in his soul? Though he'd failed to add that any soul can accept only a certain number of holes before it turns into a pit. I judged him by what then hurt me most, his seduction of little Ruth Winternitz. Now he'd thrown away the pistol for which the two women in the maize had risked their necks. As a result, something had died in me. He probably wouldn't notice.

I could hear her scream: "You don't have to worry about me. I don't want anything. I don't need anything."

Then I heard his raised voice: "You should always want something. So long as you want something there's hope for you. To want is freedom."

"What do you want from me?" she shouted. "You're selfish. Like my father. You don't care about me. You care only for yourself."

And then: "Don't say 'my' Gottlieb Faber. He's your man. A gentlemen with golden hands. Maybe at cards. Or with whores. With the women he turns into whores."

Leah's old bruises may have been joined by fresh ones. I was away from the building by then. The rain was lashing me. I didn't mind getting soaked. I was carrying my loot home under my shirt. I sensed what it was in their relationship that kept them afloat and simultaneously sank them. I walked past a solid fence behind which was a park, the officers' mess and the Commandant's office. The *Kameradschaftsheim*. At the gate to the Commandant's office stood two tall SS sentries. One pistol in the darkness could have taken care of both. The story of Goliath was both the same and a little different in every age. As was that of Samson.

I stepped into a puddle. I was thinking of the beautiful Leah from Leeuwarden and of the cinnamon eyes of little Ruth Winternitz. Of Gottlieb Faber, as if I already knew him. About how a pistol vanishes from the world, and of when the sanitary squads would come, led by the Chief Rabbi of Berlin. About the camp aristocracy, about how some were on top and some at the bottom. About how we got stirred up before being transported to the East. I hadn't heard yet about I. G. Farben, that international concern whose profits its shareholders divided among themselves even during the war, regardless of race, nationality or longitude. We didn't yet know about Zyklon B. One tin of green crystals for five hundred people. Four tins for two thousand men, women and children, healthy and sick old people, to ensure it took 15 minutes, two to make sure it didn't take longer than half an hour, for there were others waiting their turn, nine to ten thousand per day, nine to ten thousand by night, every day and every night. We didn't yet know the smoke or the stench of bodies and bones, a stench so strong it clung to the skin. I didn't want to know. Escape? Where to? Relaxation alternated with extreme punishment. Yellow caps and six-pointed stars were just the beginning. Those who helped usually ended up against the wall or on the gallows. Nothing was more unforgiving that the German race laws. I couldn't visualize 60,000 thousand people running away from the fortress ghetto. More likely they'd be massacred while still on fortress territory, somewhere near the Bohušovice meadow, where they'd counted us once, thousands of us, myself included. I thought of the meadow, of machine guns, submachine guns, small arms. Waffen-SS units in full battle dress with well-fed Alsatians on short leads. A vast basin surrounded by mountains. The dream of freedom. It occurred to me that some people were born lucky. They didn't run into an invisible wall. Into a barrier or a ditch between longing and failure.

I was wet through again and chilled from the rain.

Three

Don't regret that yesterday is yesterday
don't complain that today is today
Think of rivers, mountains, seas
and why dogs bark and horses neigh . . .

On Monday, news spread through the fortress that the next transport would be leaving. As always before a departure, a hectic search began on the black market for salamis that would keep, warm underwear, American dollars and Swiss francs, for ways of sending word to friends and relations who were not yet in the fortress and, finally, for tickets to the cellar of the Hamburg barracks and for the Firemen's House, for a performance of *Die Fledermaus* and for the *Karusel* cabaret of the German actor Kurt Geron, where they played hit tunes like "*Theresienstadt, die schönste Stadt der Welt*", "The Harlequin's Millions", "Fireflies" and others.

In the attic of the Firemen's House I ran into Vili Feld and Leah from Leeuwarden. We found places together on the long, narrow garden seats. They were playing "*Ohne Eier, ohne Butter, ohne Fett*". From afternoon until late at night, employees of the Council of Elders were delivering call-up papers for the transport. At the Firemen's House, the Hofers from Vienna sang about caviar, about bars in Grinzing and the Barrandov in

Prague, about how people are always at home in their hearts, and about how the Terezín ghetto seemed the most beautiful in Central Europe. The song had four verses. The audience applauded and insisted on an encore, everyone was smiling. During the intermission, foreign currency dealings went on, in groups or in twos; rings, gold and diamonds changed hands. For a while, at least, we found consolation. Escaped into the realm of fantasy. A reminder of what had been and might be again.

Leah was sitting between Vili and me.

"At least this has some truth to it," he said.

"Two hours' worth," she remarked.

She smelled nice. Perhaps she was naked again under her dress. I was flooded with excitement. I shoved my hands into my pockets. My heart was racing.

In her porcelain complexion there was vagueness, maybe mystery, gaiety one moment and pain or uncertainty the next about what might happen.

Perhaps some of the people in the audience prayed; they felt loved, they breathed, Leah was shaped in their image but filled with anger, venality, rebellion and impotence. Here she had learned not to believe anything or anybody, perhaps not even herself.

"Before every transport I feel as if someone has torn my clothes off," she said. Then in a small voice, to me, she added: "Light makes me guilty and darkness forgives me."

"Today riddles are only permitted on the stage," Vili said. He smiled at me. "Nothing is easier for a woman in danger than to seduce a man."

He was thinking about something else. I thought I could guess what it was: how to get Leah and himself off the transport. He had his ways, from the waist down. They were playing "South of the Alps". Was she perhaps thinking they could buy themselves off?

Her smile was beautiful. No-one could have guessed her life was on the line. (As was everyone else's.) She smelled of soap. Beneath the layers of her ideas and memories, her intentions (which she kept to herself), she was like a closed clam. A pearl that loses its gleam when someone touches it. In her features there was reconciliation, fatigue. I could sense her resignation. Was she thinking of her father, her mother, the court when she stood naked in the yard before her envious teachers? She was laughing nervously and applauding. "Here Comes the Grub" – a two-year-old Terezín song to the tune of "Come with Me to Varazdin" from Lehar's operetta *Countess Maritza*. And "Terezín, attention!", the march of the ghetto guard. Leah liked "The Two Oxen" and "As if", while Vili preferred "Transport" and "Musical Accompaniment", a parody of a hit by Rosita-Serrano to the music of Freddy Raymond.

"It's all very international," I said.

"Like everything here over the past three years," said Vili. "Even if a bunch of backwoodsmen arrived here, they'd leave as cosmopolitans. We're all leaving as different persons from when we arrived."

"You haven't left yet," I said.

I remembered what Vili had said by the latrine after he'd dropped his pistol into it. Every woman is enveloped in mystery.

Suddenly I felt my hand in Leah's.

"These people are not defeated. They're still laughing."

She drank in the features of the singers and the actors. She perceived their strength or energy, the way they turned songs and words into movement and imagination, fear into courage, uncertainty into companionship, into awareness of a common destiny, a secret resistance. She immersed herself in a different mood from the one she'd been in when she'd arrived, in a warming stream created by the spectators on the wooden benches. Heat radiated from her.

The skin of her palm was soft as moss. The skin of a warm animal. With her other hand she was holding Vili's. Her legs touched my thigh on the left and Vili's on the right. She was sharing herself even though we didn't wish to share her.

"We're still breathing," Vili said.

There was silver in her eyes, like a full moon. She let go of Vili's hand and smoothed her skirt over her knees.

The Hofers, husband and wife, were singing. Their songs, composed at the last minute, were all mockery, rebellion and, eventually, sentimentality. Nostalgia. A few people applauded with tears in their eyes.

I thought about fidelity. About Vili's amorous adventures. Did everyone get what they deserved? I wished Leah could read my thoughts.

"What's going to happen?" she whispered.

I only needed to touch her hand to realize what I hadn't touched yet. I was trembling. The world around me was losing its threat. I could have lain down on the track along which a locomotive was going to haul cattle trucks, the ones in which we'd all be travelling East, down to the last person, and I wouldn't have trembled. But now I did. I was flooded by song, by the saxophones, the accordions and the trumpets. The actors and singers had both the tawdriness and the nobility of the time in which we lived. I clung to the idea of getting back at

Vili, even though the transport would be leaving in two days, on Wednesday, probably in the morning, and we wouldn't have much time.

"One day we'll make up for all this," Vili said.

I thought of what Leah had said by the dormer window in her attic about identity. About how it killed her to be alone. As if she didn't exist. She refused to become a pawn in a game that had no name and whose results were recorded by self-appointed umpires. Perhaps she was glad, in a perverse way, that she was going on the transport. She felt like her father, kept here at the expense of someone she didn't even know. She refused to be a victim, but also to be responsible for the sacrifice of somebody else.

She held my hand until the performance ended.

In my mind I whispered to her that for me she was naked even in her clothes. Next to her I was also naked, like Adam with Eve. The performance went on for more than an hour. The actors earned endless applause. For a while people forgot (or tried to forget) that the day after tomorrow they would be off to Poland.

Four

"His best advice was: Don't give advice to anyone."

– Inscription on a shell

The following day, it was Tuesday afternoon, I found a message from Leah in Room 16 on L 218, where I was living with Adler in the Boys' Home. She would be alone that night in the attic she shared with Vili. (I could have found it blindfolded.) She'd be glad if I would come. The message ended with the words "I'm waiting. My father's not far away now. One trip by goods train." She had folded the note into a five-by-five-centimetre square. I wondered briefly if someone wasn't setting a trap for me.

She also wrote that I might be interested in what the tarot cards were predicting for me. She confused me with her final sentence: "For the second night now, I've dreamed of you. With you." I didn't want to show the note to Adler, but eventually I did. (He grinned.) I was ready to go even if it was a trap. I could sense her body in every word. (Only later did she say she was a gift that couldn't be opened.) This was the last evening before the transport. Adler and I had already received our summonses. I wondered if she had.

The moon was up. It was a pleasant night. A bluish mist filled the air. The mountains to the north were disappearing.

It was eight minutes to eight: I could just manage to get to Leah's place but would not be able to return to L 218, even if I wanted to. Except in the early morning. The Germans had announced a total curfew for the night. No exceptions. As before every transport, patrols of the Waffen-SS and the gendarmerie were increased to reinforce the Jewish *Ghetto-Wache*. (Adler thought I was mad. Had I already packed my things? We had a margarine box, tied up with guitar strings to hold all our clothes. We knew we wouldn't need much. The most important items we were wearing already. It was best to take warm things. Adler made me a gift of his extra tracksuit, to be worn under my clothes; he said it was too big for him.)

I passed some of the old people on the stairs in Leah's building. I smelled their stench and felt their glances on my back. They were dragging empty suitcases and boxes down the stairs, along with their own bodies. Some of them had already put on their mountain or ski boots with thick woollen socks and extra warm underwear (saved from confiscation for the *Winterhilfe*) and had wrapped themselves in scarves. I knocked at the attic door. She was standing close to it.

"Good evening."

She was alone.

"I hope this isn't a mistake," I added.

"Depends on what you've come for."

Was she inviting me to kiss her? Or was this just a friendly welcome? I was overcome by nervousness. Her lips were half opened. Her skin was luminous. She smelled of soap. I knew she was naked under her clothes.

It didn't matter what I said.

"I've come for a good reason."

"My father used to say that people didn't make mistakes, they were just learning all the time." She smiled. "What's new?"

"Nothing much," I said.

"Glad to hear it."

"Everything's fine."

"What could still surprise us?"

"Are you on it?"

"Yes. And you?"

"Both of us."

I was surprised that of all people she'd have mentioned her father. Was she about to commit some sort of betrayal? "You, you," I thought. I was aware of her face, her eyes and lips, her porcelain skin, her long legs, her breasts and her sex. I breathed in her perfume. It was everything that makes a woman's body fragrant. I felt as if real life would only start when I touched her. She must have sensed my nervousness and the way I was trying to stay calm. I must have looked hungry. Around her I felt something I had never felt before. She sighed.

"There's no other news," she said.

"No news is good news, isn't it?"

"I don't even need to know where we are going. There are lots of things I don't know. Where will I sleep? Or eat? With whom? What will happen to me? What won't? Who'll wake us in the mornings? And how? Wolves? Foxes? The wind? Rats, as here? Hunger? Some new disease?"

"The cold," I said. "Best put on boots. Warm stockings, warm underwear. Better two pairs of gloves than one. As for the rest, I'm not bothered."

We didn't know about the five crematoria at Auschwitz-Birkenau. About the pits and the mass graves. About the largest and most efficient camp in the world. About Zyklon B. What we imagined didn't have to be true.

"I don't want to be serious."

My throat felt tight.

"Nor sentimental."

Then she added: "There's one thing you can get drunk on and yet remain sober."

And finally: "I'm afraid of crowds."

I could imagine where she was in her mind. What she knew that Adler and I didn't.

"You, me," she said. "The Germans. Not one cattle truck less. They're thorough. Like ants, if ants resembled humans, wore green SS uniforms, worshipped the swastika and had submachine guns or rifles over their shoulders."

I remained silent. I didn't want to share her serious mood; I had other anxieties. No-one doubted the Germans' thoroughness, fastidiousness, accuracy or punctuality. I sensed that she was sad.

The window was open. Bluish moonlight entered the room. A wind was blowing; tomorrow we'd be travelling towards it. It carried the smell of the mountains. On the tracks they were assembling the train. We could hear the clanging of the cattle trucks. By morning they'd have hitched up 50 trucks for 5,000 people. Half of them men, half of them women, all able to work. (There was talk of the old people going by the next transport.) Two engines, one in front, the other at the back. On their flanks a white "V" for *Viktoria*. We knew about these German trains by now. The haze of the journey – from somewhere to somewhere else. That strange feeling when you see a train, whether it is standing still or moving or disappearing into the distance. Cattle trucks that had seen things. The taste of steam, smoke and soot from the funnel of the locomotive. The thought of a journey meant a change. Regardless of the destination. Meanwhile, there was the darkness, the ceaseless rain, the mud. The continual greyness. In Leah's eyes was the eagerness that reminded me of our first meeting and our first goodbye. Her smooth skin, the circles under her eyes, her bare arms. She must have had a long day, and she looked tired. Everybody was tired. Or maybe she was wrestling with uncomfortable thoughts. There were 60,000 people doing that in the fortress.

She was pleased I had come. She gave me one of her beautiful smiles. I didn't want to feel like a conqueror before the fact. That might result in defeat.

Leah closed her eyes. She was listening to voices. Probably not just from the rail yard or from the old people's home. Was she hearing echoes of those who'd left for the East before us? (Later, when I returned to this in my mind, there was a mystery in it. She said: "You'll leave me just as we all leave someone.") On the inside walls of the cattle trucks were those messages and clues about gas. Only some of our leaders understood them then. They didn't know how to deal with them. Where could 60,000 powerless people run to? Who'd give them shelter? They'd provoke a massacre the likes of which the Czech lands had never experienced. Preceded by the despair of mothers with children, of helpless fathers without weapons or organization, and of even more helpless old and sick people. This conjured up horrendous visions. So our leaders who knew kept silent. They saw to it that the transports left without confusion. No-one wanted to change places with them. If Goering had said that he wouldn't like to be a Jew in Germany, then it was even worse to be a Jewish leader, a member of the Council of Elders, during that night from Tuesday to Wednesday. (And on other similar days and nights.)

I tried to retrieve my carefree mood. I wondered where Vili Feld was. I stayed by the door. She was still looking out of the window into the dark.

"Last night in the fortress," she said.

"Looks like it."

"No regrets."

"That depends."

"Done your packing?"

"How about you?"

She nodded towards the baggage by the door. "Vili went out at seven to the Central Registry. He's not going to risk coming back after the curfew. It's better to be in the East than to be beaten up here or executed in the Lesser Fortress."

"Is he with Gottlieb Faber?"

She just looked at me. "Gottlieb Faber has it all behind him."

"They've locked him up? Or has he left already?"

I thought about what might have happened to him. Had he been caught as he was buying foreign currency? Had one of his own people denounced him? Or had somebody settled a score with him because he'd dispatched a relative in place of one of his protégés? How long could the pitcher go to the well before it broke?

"He hid our index cards three times. For others he did it ten times or more. I don't know exactly what he got in exchange. Or how much he did unselfishly or on a whim, or just because he was able to. He was more complex than he seemed. He was neither blind nor stupid. For those he saved, there was always someone else who had to go. Some people don't know about this, others are irritated by it, but there are a lot of us who don't care any longer. Like yourself, I'm alive only because someone else went off to the East. I can only guess whether they've already been killed instead of me. I don't know how he got away with it so often. More and more he reminded me of my father."

It struck me that she was speaking of Gottlieb Faber in the past tense.

"Wouldn't you hide your best friend's card?"

"I don't know. Who wouldn't want to save his own skin?"

"He swallowed a potassium cyanide pill."

Getting hold of potassium cyanide wasn't difficult in the fortress. It was a quick death. Hallucinations, then spasms of which you were no longer aware.

She'd said it in a matter-of-fact way to shock me.

Gottlieb Faber had played with destiny just like the Germans. Had he managed to keep his hands clean while deciding who'd live and who'd die? He hadn't condemned anybody off his own bat. He'd merely attached himself to a system that was sending people to the East and murdering them there. Had his time come sooner than he'd expected? Had he known more than the rest of us? Had he feared something more than others? He had been one of those in the know.

"Everyone's saving his own skin. You can't swim across a dirty river without getting dirty yourself. He was no saint. Hardly anyone in his place would be."

Then she went on: "Last Wednesday he talked to me about suicide. How women can be sick to death of everything but cope with it. He was older than me. By 37 years. Too clever not to see the difference between real and faked pleasure. He had an insatiable interest in the flesh – right up to the last moment. He laughed at me. To him everything had to do with the body. He was frightened on his own."

Leah had tied her golden hair back with a black ribbon. In her blue eyes there was fear or a request. Echoes of some ancient joy and sorrow. She disguised this with her porcelain smile. Suddenly I knew that her smile was a façade. There was horror in her eyes which, but for her 18 years and her beauty, would have made her like those old women next door. She had nothing to hold on to.

"He hated his race. I'd never met a person who minded his origin or religion every bit as much as the enemies whom he despised. Gottlieb Faber minded what he was. He seemed blind, deaf and dumb towards everything and everybody he disliked."

She saw that I needed an explanation. I wondered what shady deals Gottlieb Faber had had with Vili.

"He knew how to get people to do what he wanted them to do."

I thought about this. It wasn't as distasteful as it had seemed at first. She saw things in shorthand. I sensed what made the festive everyday, the serious ridiculous for her.

"He didn't have to do it."

Those big blue eyes. The dark circles under them.

"We are like sheep. That sergeant of yours was right."

Gottlieb Faber must still have been on her mind.

"You can't win every card game. You've got to learn to lose without batting an eyelid. On one occasion he lost his shirt. They thought he'd gone to pawn something. He came back an hour later. He'd been giving blood."

Then she added: "Some people like living on the edge."

"He maintained decorum," I remarked. "He bluffed."

"He reminded me of my father."

Gottlieb Faber had described the ghetto and the Nazis' anti-Jewish war: the fortress, he'd said, was like an elephant's foot probed by a blind man.

"The Council of Elders are chess players. They play without preparation, hastily, without tactics or strategy. Faber compared them to the villagers who followed the Pied Piper of Hamelin. He watched the clock on the wall. Each tick filled him with horror. Are you in a hurry?"

"We've got all night," I said.

The moonlight gilded her eyebrows. I wondered what would happen if Vili came back. But he'd hardly be likely to settle his business with the Council of Elders in an hour.

"Don't be afraid," she said.

"I'm not."

Two vulcanite cases stood by the door. Her tarot cards were set out on the packing crate, just as when I had been there on Sunday. I thought of the cattle trucks. On some of them, on the sliding doors, the SS chalked the letters "RU" (Return Undesirable).

Gottlieb Faber had thought of the Germans in the Commandant's office and of their superiors in Berlin as croupiers standing behind a gigantic roulette wheel. The bank, the croupiers, the Germans won. Faber played the game several times. He didn't stand a chance of winning. An escapee from Auschwitz-Birkenau who'd made it through the selection while the rest went straight to the gas chamber, and who had returned to Terezín, told a few people what was in store for them. They agonized over what to do. One of them, Leo Baeck, the former Chief Rabbi of Berlin, believed that to live in expectation of one's death was harder than death itself. Gottlieb Faber agreed. He took his potassium cyanide.

Weren't we, quite aside from that German roulette, also playing our own game?

"I don't judge him. Faber's train has come to a halt. He pulled the emergency brake."

I went over to the crate with the tarot cards.

"What did the cards show you?"

"A journey."

"A train?"

"The day when I'll be old."

The books on the shelf shone in the twilight.

"I understand why they burn books. They are struggling with a greatness they cannot bear. They can glorify themselves only by reducing everything else."

Kafka, who reminded her of a sad prophet, would be left to the mice and earwigs.

"He never overcame his childhood fear," she said about Vili. "Fear of his mother, who mourned his older brother. He didn't break free of the horrors of childhood."

Then she said: "I'm taking a book of Dutch fairy tales with me. I got them when I was in the first form and learning to read, on my sixth birthday. Jan de Hartog, *The Glory of Holland*. He ran away to sea when he was ten. His father, a pastor, got him back, but the boy ran away again and worked as a deckhand. He rose from common sailor to captain and began to write. The Nazis were after him. He hid in an old people's home, disguised as an old woman."

She looked at my greased boots. "I'm leaving my golden-heeled slippers to the rats," she said.

"Isn't it getting late?" I said.

She must have known that I hadn't come so she could tell me what she was reading.

She looked at me as if she was the one who'd run here across the fortress, not me. She seemed different from how she'd been a little earlier. A porcelain beauty that could be broken. She was looking at the four rows of cards, eight in each row.

"The first row shows the sadness of love. The sufferings of the body from the waist down and waist up. The second involves the soul. The third signifies regrets. Rivers and darkness, distances, green forests and blue sky. The land where you were born. The fourth is nostalgia for lost people."

"How can the cards know all that?"

"There's a simplicity that shines out of the most complex things."

Had she decided to be unfaithful to Vili in order to punish him? Was that why she had asked me if I had come for a good reason, because she herself had chosen a bad one?

Did she need someone to confirm her existence? What about the bruises on her arms? Was she afraid she might meet her father in the East?

"Rumours came from the East about gas, rumours which Gottlieb Faber kept quiet for a long time. About the extermination of families. About slave labour under conditions beyond compare with ancient Egypt, Babylon or Rome. They have a plan to exterminate millions of children, old people, sick ones and healthy ones, men and women. They're doing what no-one in history has yet achieved. The man in charge was Heydrich, killed by the Czechs. They want to kill us all. It's only a question of time."

"Why would they do that?"

"Because they can."

"He didn't tell anyone else?"

"He convinced himself that there is no God. Anybody can do anything. The Ten Commandments are a joke. In what way would telling have helped? Would people turn against armed German soldiers? What about the children? The women? The old people? Who can talk of morality in an immoral world? The SS men wipe their behinds with the Old Testament."

I suppressed the desire to open my arms and embrace her without speaking. I tried to make myself brave and simultaneously felt ashamed. I didn't want to talk about Gottlieb Faber or what the German soldiers wiped their behinds with.

"Maybe they are just trying to scare us. They enjoy horrifying us. They believe they are strong, victorious and clever. Superior to us."

"You think they can't do it?"

"What else did the cards say about me?"

"You have a friend who turns what is good into something less good and what is bad into something worse."

"Suppose I am like that myself?"

"The cards say the opposite. You deny yourself a lot of things. As if they didn't exist. There is joy in you that you are ready to share. You'd like to live life as if it were a feast. You walk on glowing embers. Considering your experience, you are trusting. If you haven't actually lost, you consider that a victory. You have one foot in the world of dreams."

"You could say that about everybody."

After a while she began to speak about Gottlieb Faber again. I was neither a little lamb nor a thug. Like Vili, I believed in situational morality, not morality handed down by God. I didn't have to call what I believed in the law of the jungle; this *was* a jungle. Here things were concentrated like condensed milk in a tin.

"Faber has three children who are on tomorrow's transport. I don't know his wife. Supposedly he hasn't touched her in five years. Each one of his children is different. The oldest is a crybaby, always complaining and whingeing. The middle one is a clown who finds everything funny. The youngest is a dear. Everyone loves him. His wife didn't understand how she could have such different children by the same man. And he didn't understand how he could have married her. Physical contact disgusts her. She's like my grandmother."

We could hear the old people. They were dragging a cabin trunk along the corridor.

"They can't carry anything."

"Did you give them something?"

"Nothing much."

I could imagine what she had given away.

"You're pretty."

"You've said that before."

"It's true."

"Thanks."

"I've got something for you," I said.

I started unbuttoning my shirt. A smile appeared on her lips.

"According to my father, a man and a woman shouldn't exchange gifts before they are married." She laughed. "When my father was with me, he was a different person. One of the most popular horse vets. I don't understand how he could have betrayed everyone he knew."

"Did he know the people he put on his list?"

"Which is worse? To know a person you're having killed, or not to know him? To know he went to the East in your place? I'm trying to visualize the people he sold. How the Gestapo selected them."

"What did your father look like?"

"I knew you'd ask me that. A little like Vili, and a tiny little bit like Faber and yourself. I'm not like him."

"Why did he do it?"

"You know what they say about opportunity. He was not the stuff that saints are made of."

I thought about her story of the jockey and the blind horse. Leah's father, the vet, was the first to spot its dilated pupils. For a long time the horse didn't collide with anything, even when he was not with his groom. He knew where his trough was, where the stable door was, and the windows through which the sun shone. When he was being groomed, he'd turn his head like any other horse. He was not bothered by hens or sparrows in the hay, or by mice and rats, or even by the small dogs that chased them out. To look at him, no-one would have guessed he was blind. He had no idea where he was.

I was thinking of the legacy Leah's father had left her. Mine hadn't left me anything. Wasn't that better? My fingers were on my second shirt button. She was watching them.

"I dreamed I was holding a spoon of honey; the honey was spilling from it but the spoon remained full. Then the honey began to disappear."

My fingers froze on my third button.

"Vili keeps having a dream from his childhood. When he was a little boy he wouldn't go to sleep until his mother whispered to him: 'Goodnight. Sleep well. I love you. Everything will be all right.' That was before his brother died. After that she no longer said it. For his mother, everything died with his brother."

Her beauty was different from that celebrated by the Germans. I hadn't encountered this before. In her features, her eyes and her physical presence there were tenderness and sadness about the passing of time. This was the opposite of the body cult proclaimed by the SS men in the Commandant's office, who got up at 3.30 in the morning to run their 10 or 15 kilometres, box, fence and work out in the gym before daybreak. The opposite of what one saw on posters or the front pages of periodicals like the pilots' journal *Der Adler*. A kind of health that exterminated the feeble-minded and infirm as a way of enhancing itself, a strength that manifested itself in the killing of the weak. I sometimes wondered what they would do with their war-wounded, those who'd lost a leg or an eye.

The old people reminded us of their presence.

At times I found it difficult to hear Leah. She was almost talking to herself. Was she testing or tormenting me?

"Something else the cards told me about you. You want to cross a river."

"You've got beautiful hair," I said, already with my shirt half unbuttoned.

"A lot of people know what I am better than I do myself," she said. "Or what I was before Vili, or next to Gottlieb Faber."

I was perplexed. "Do you hate him?" I asked.

"Do you?"

"One day I'll tell you what he did to me. It involved a 16-year-old girl."

"I'm worse off," she said. "I hate my father even though I'm sorry for him."

"As a boy I thought Vili must be rich," I said.

I didn't want to talk about her father.

When I was 15, Vili had seemed wealthy to me, though I had no idea – apart from fairy tales – how the really rich behaved. (I never got anywhere close to them. And it didn't look as if this would change.) I had watched the way he spoke, how he dressed and moved, whom he talked to and how, whom he ignored. I had explored his territory, his values (without calling them that), whom he would meet, whom he'd avoid and how he ate.

He'd often spoken of Darwin. Was that a clue? In some respects, no doubt. How he'd got what he got, even though he might lose it later. What he did, considering the circumstances, to regain it. What he took seriously and what he didn't.

Some answers I found at once, most of them not until later. There was more and more of Darwin in it. The jungle, where the strong devour the weak in order to survive.

"Some people in Leeuwarden thought I came from a million-aire's family, though nothing was further from the truth. My mother enjoyed creating that impression."

"You look rich," I said, and it wasn't a lie.

"Appearance and reality are stepsisters," she said. "I probably have that from my mother."

"There are a few former millionaires here. In Prague I

thought Vili was one of them. Some people give that impression without even trying."

"You are too kind," she smiled. "Some people here act like they're rich. Many pretend they were."

I didn't want her to be so serious. Things were going in a different direction from what I wanted.

I was flooded with desire. Her whispering, her words. What she radiated, the waves I was receiving, like the sun's rays or the touch of twilight. It almost didn't matter what she was talking about.

Was she, as she stood next to me, thinking of her father who'd be hanged after the war if he survived the East and returned home to be tried? Of the baker who didn't know what was more valuable – his flour and bread, or the gold he made from them, which he plastered into the wall to collect after the war? Usury, the black market, I couldn't have cared less about these things. I was a fan of the Ghetto Swingers, who sent their jazz arrangements to Prague, where they were played until 1944 in the Vltava Café. (Until, that is, the Germans banned the Czechs from dancing.)

I wanted to have her. To embrace her. To feel her so close that it couldn't be closer. To fuse with her. To rise with her above everything that disturbed her, so that only the now, she and I, were left. I had no words for it. Only an adolescent's nervousness. I had no time to reflect on how certainty could arise from uncertainty, self-assurance from anxiety. Everything in me at that moment was selfish. Yet at the same time unselfish and soft, like a cry for help. I felt like I – as once I had done – was hanging by my hands under a viaduct while a goods train passed overhead. I heard the roar above me. It filled my ears and brain. If I made a mistake, I'd fall and be killed.

I knew I had been born lucky. Whenever I'd got into trouble, I'd got out with no more than ruffled feathers. I'd learned to be a survivor even before they'd deported us to the fortress. I knew, even at home, what hunger was. I'd had no need, like Vili or Gottlieb Faber, to save myself at the expense of anyone else. I was not consumed by a wish to feel more important than those around me. But I didn't believe it was my destiny to be a loser.

I'd come to measure myself against Vili Feld, Leah's lover and companion. I recalled what he had told me about her. It wasn't only Gottlieb Faber that she had managed to twist round her little finger. He'd taught her to look at reality differently.

For a moment she wore the expression of a person beyond help. In the dusk her skin was like a rose covered with pollen. Later, her cheeks were like peaches dented by fingerprints. The seriousness in her eyes confused me. Something that momentarily disappeared and then reappeared. As if she was present and yet not.

"A girl is a seed," she said. "It seeks fertile soil for itself."

I kept silent.

"Without love the body is just a few chunks of raw meat."

I still managed to keep silent.

"I don't know many people I'd want to stay with."

"You've got lovely hair."

She caressed me with her glance.

"Lots of people would like to cut women's hair off. I wrote to you that I dreamed about you. Somebody asked me how you were. I said I couldn't answer that, though I could have done. You were sitting on a river bank, fishing. There were currents there, but your float didn't even move. You crossed over to the other bank, but you didn't catch anything there either. That's how he is, I said. You got used to one bank. Then you crossed over and remembered the first. When you got back you saw that the first bank, to which you'd got used, wasn't as beautiful as you'd thought when you were on the other, and that the far bank, to which you couldn't get used, wasn't so bad. Then I dreamed that we were together in Buenos Aires. I was looking for you at an agreed place by some brothel, but in the end we didn't find each other."

"Thanks. Next time I'll wait for you." Again I said: "You've got lovely hair."

"I like wearing it long. Before we leave tomorrow, I'd like to cut it off. Before they cut it off for me. Women are fonder of their hair than men can understand. When I look at other women's hair I'm glad I have mine. I wouldn't like to lose it."

"Why should you lose it?"

"Because of what Gottlieb Faber said before he swallowed his pill."

She had aged – or felt she was growing old.

"I know better things than the body," she said softly.

She looked at me with knowing blue eyes, eyes questioning without demanding a reply.

"When a man wants to get a woman he'll do anything to win her, and once he's had her he feels an urge to humiliate her. In men, longing mixes with brutality. Satisfaction with revenge."

I didn't know why she was saying this to me. Didn't it apply to women as well? Was she drawing me into the world of Vili and Gottlieb Faber, where, at the same time, she didn't want me?

"I'll go wherever you ask me to," I said.

Should I ask how she got her bruises?

"Be different," she said.

"How?"

"Different from him."

"In what?"

"In everything."

She seemed as distant from me as I felt close to her.

"D'you want to talk to me about love?" she asked, softly. "It's in your cards."

"I don't know," I said, just as softly.

She remained in the dusk – like nightfall, before the dark closes in.

"Love is an angel or a devil like ourselves. Maybe it can't be anything else. Love is what we were, what we shall be. Or what we won't ever be. What we don't know about ourselves. What nobody knows."

It was nice to hear the word *love* from her lips. It occurred to me that even if she slept with me, she wouldn't feel she was being unfaithful. She saw betrayal differently.

"You probably don't know what love is," she said. "You know what the body is."

She turned her head to the side. Her hair covered half her face.

"Everything about you is pretty – your hair, your face, your legs, your hands. You're a beautiful girl."

"I'm ashamed to say that work ruins your hands and nails."

In her mind she turned in another direction. Then she said: "To be pretty means – up to a point – to be free. But for how long?"

In Leeuwarden she had known a goldsmith. He was afraid of perfection. On every piece of jewellery he made a little mistake.

She was listening to the wind. Somewhere in the distance it was raining. Behind a curtain of clouds, the invisible mountains lay like naked women in the dark.

Then she said: "I got married. This morning we went to the rabbi. He looked at me the way you did when you came here on Sunday. He said that the most important thing is to understand another person so you can understand yourself. He confirmed that if we survived deportation and returned from the East, our marriage would be legal."

"You wanted that?" I breathed. Suddenly I understood her restraint. "And Vili?" (Was I the first person she'd told?)

I wondered why she'd asked me to come. Had she lost her mind? (That was what Adler had asked me.) Surely she must have known that after the curfew I couldn't get back to L 218. Had she acted on a whim or out of loneliness or despair? I tried hard not to betray my thoughts. I was glad it was almost dark. I still couldn't make sense of her.

"He likes my long legs. My face, my body, my eyes, the way we make love. He's got a name for everything. Sometimes he'll tell me I have an angel's face, that he is with me because of how I look. The time will come when he lets me go. Or when he finds me somebody else, like Gottlieb Faber, so he can get rid of me."

"And you?"

"I'd hoped that he'd have only me. That he knew I was on his side. He let me think that he was on my side."

I was furious. This wasn't what I had expected. I was asking myself questions instead of acting. Had she invited me as a witness to her wedding, a belated one? Did she want to have two weddings? Or expunge the first with a second one?

"I'm afraid of that second life together. Of what he might do to me if I am no longer pretty."

It occurred to me later that, thanks to Gottlieb Faber, she knew more than the rest of us. Loneliness was destroying her like a disease.

"If you are a girl you don't have much choice. About sharing yourself with someone."

What I said suddenly sounded more adult. It had lost the awkwardness that Adler and I used as a disguise. I was surprised at the way I spoke. I was more serious. I concealed my disappointment.

"I'm a married woman. Isn't that what every girl wants?"

She looked towards the door. She was listening to the old people who'd be setting out with their luggage at daybreak to make sure they were on time. Cases and rucksacks were their most solid possessions. Employees of the Council of Elders would come at dawn to help them; others would perhaps be helped by their relatives, by their grown-up children; yet others would be carried because they wouldn't be able to make it to the loading ramp or into the cattle trucks on their own. Still others would have their suitcases stolen. Few of the old folk would manage to sleep in order to gather strength for the journey. Except those who fell asleep and didn't wake up again. "They go through their years as if through muddy water," she said about them. "They look back even if they're going forward. The past is a wall to them. When you live miserably, you think you've lived a long time. No matter how old you are."

I waited for a while. The old people fell silent.

"I've seen them die." Then she added: "Old age is hideous. It waits for everybody lucky enough not to have been killed."

"Why did you get married?"

"It's a fake marriage. We're not talking about wedded bliss."

Each word meant three other words, and every three meant another nine. In the summer they'd had ants here, her grandmother called them pharaohs, and in summer and winter bedbugs, cockroaches and all kinds of vermin. I didn't want to talk or even think about mice and rats. I knew why there weren't any dogs or cats. Fellows like Adler made no distinction between kinds of meat. To eat the Germans' cats felt like a kind of resistance.

She was gazing towards the darkening mountains. At the low clouds. At the dusk turning black in the east and becoming night.

"In winter the ants freeze to death," she said.

"I've brought you a rose," I said and finally pulled out the stem I had under my shirt. It was a red rose, forced to open by the warmth of my body and slightly squashed. Leah looked at me with her porcelain smile.

"My birthday isn't until tomorrow, but you probably didn't know that." She looked at the rose as though it were an entire dozen. "I'll keep it here overnight." (She kissed the faded petals.) "In the morning I'll get you to keep it for me."

I understood. She put the rose in a soda-water bottle. The evening no longer had any shadows. It was quite dark. "They say that nightingales and women love roses." Then she added: "If you are given flowers, you mustn't give them to anyone else; it's bad luck."

"You're the first recipient."

"Where do they grow here?"

"In the garden of Waffen-SS Heindl."

"How did you manage it?"

"I moved quickly."

"Weren't you afraid?"

"I'm always afraid," I smiled. "Sometimes I get bellyache."

"I know the feeling," she laughed.

"I let myself down on a rope from the third bastion. It's quite near to his villa. It's a big garden."

"Hasn't Heindl got a dog?"

"Took him out riding."

"Well done!"

"It was fun."

"You think so?"

My shirt was open to my waist. I saw her breasts move in the flashes of moonlight. Everything was going my way again – in spite of the surprise she had given me. I felt that nicer part of excitement, an anxiety that didn't hurt, a kind of fear that wasn't frightening. The spirituality that pervades the body and the physical element that inspires. The calm that pervades the storm and the tumultuousness within calm.

She lit the candle on the packing crate. The wick was short. She turned up a few cards. The attic reminded me of a boat. The cases by the door looked worn in the candlelight. They'd been used a lot. A rumour had gone round that the less conspicuous your luggage was, the less tempting it was to steal it. (Except for the Germans.)

"The Jews have become a nation of packers." She'd followed my glance. "We'd travelled quite a bit even before this. He's taking his two favourite cashmere pullovers. He wears them next to his skin, without a shirt or vest. He had three. He gave me the blue one. I'll be wearing it tomorrow."

"The stars are shining," I said.

"Mist."

"I love the mountains," I added. "Sometimes even the mist."

I thought of how tomorrow Vili and Leah would put their cashmere pullovers on over their bare skin.

"There isn't much light. The summer is short here."

"Isn't it the same in Holland?"

"The water stays in the valleys and plains, it's humid and it rains a lot. The whole country is nothing but work and dykes and the horror that the sea might swallow us up. It's true that you even get used to the gallows."

The moon looked like a round fish. The stars shone brightly. She walked over to the door on the other side of which we could hear the old people and turned the key in the lock. She left the key in the door. She didn't have to explain anything now. I thought of Vili Feld. Was I betraying him as he had betrayed me with Ruth Winternitz? As Leah was betraying him? Was infidelity an ocean in which we were all swimming? I amused myself with the vision of me climbing out of the dormer window and sliding down the drainpipe so as to present myself punctually for transport in the morning.

I saw Leah's body in the dark – her hips, her long legs.

"I'd like to know why the Germans are doing what they are doing to us. They know how it will end." She was thinking of what Gottlieb Faber had told her.

"They won't kill everybody," I said.

"Three girls I know were raped," said Leah. "The first one

– that was still in Holland – was raped by a businessman, an Arab. He was a great one for proverbs: a man is the son of his day, life without drink is a dried-up river bed, a bee that doesn't give honey . . . and so on. He said that pleasure's day was short and tore her clothes off her. She was having her period. He didn't mind. At least she wouldn't get pregnant. She didn't know whether to laugh or cry. The second one was raped by a Pole. She'd invited him to her place and joked that a girl with a bad reputation had the most visitors. With some men it's better not to joke. The third one was raped by Germans. They'd come for some water. She wished she was ugly. They advised her to lock her door next time. They said they could tell a virgin at a hundred paces. One of them had singed eyebrows and no lashes, with eyes set high in his forehead."

I cleared my throat. I looked at her in the misty darkness with its stars and faint moonlight. I wondered where she'd be on her nineteenth birthday. Why had she told me about those rapes? There was more within her than I could understand.

"In the Central Registry at the Magdeburg barracks," she said, "the index-card boxes are guarded by new people from the Council of Elders. Austrians, people from Bohemia and Moravia and from Germany, to make sure they're evenly represented in the transports. They've got Dutch people there. They want to share injustice justly. Vili is there, looking for someone he knows."

This wasn't the first Council of Elders to do the undoable. It was impossible to protect the unprotectable interests of one's dear ones and simultaneously obey the unbending orders of the Commandant's office.

The candlelight was playing over Leah's features. She spread her fingers above the flame. Was she trying to see how much heat she could bear? Was pain some sort of yardstick for her? The little flame danced in the breeze. She leaned against the brick wall. She was looking at the rose in the bottle.

I gazed out of the window.

"You shouldn't count the stars," she said. "He who counts the stars three times in a row must die."

"I was told that he who breaks an apple in two three times in a row will become invincible."

"If you leave the door open behind you three times in a house where someone has died, another person will die."

She looked into the flame. We sat down on boxes over which she'd thrown some blankets, our backs to the wall. The packing crate with the cards stood in the middle. I looked at the cards in the darkness. Clothes, underwear, aces and numbers.

"What are you thinking about?" I asked.

"A man I knew in the RAF. He took me to a concert. A piano recital given by a 14-year-old girl. I envied her talent. And I'm thinking of my father. Of the cruelty of relatives. What are you thinking of?"

"Of how you kissed me when I was leaving last time. It made my head spin. Of how we held hands at the Firemen's House, of you inviting me here."

She kissed me. I felt the softness and wetness of her lips. A warmth without equal.

"Not yet," she said. "We've got the whole night." Then she added: "The body is the easiest part." And finally: "What do you want, apart from what you want?"

"Tell me about the sea," I said.

"Before we left Leeuwarden, three days before the transport

to Westerborg, my father took me to the beach. He tried to convince me that I had my whole life ahead of me. He didn't want to miss saying what one says to daughters as they grow up. Before they're introduced into society. Then we picked up our bags and left."

"But isn't it true?"

"Some of it. You believe that I still have my whole life ahead of me?"

"At least something, if not everything. You're 18."

"Who counts after 18?"

"So far everything's come out all right for me. I'm quite looking forward to what lies ahead. The journey. A foreign country. New people. Change."

"You've got what I'm missing."

"If we had the time, I'd have you meet a few teachers who have told me I'd come to a bad end. Adler and I live with the problem students."

"Why haven't I got any joy in me?"

"You know things that Adler and I don't," I said to cheer her up just as she, without knowing it, was cheering me up.

She smiled. "Could you stay with anyone for long?"

"I've had no-one to try it with."

"I have. It doesn't work. No-one's explained to me why. Maybe it's better not to tie oneself to anyone. He's with me as long as I sleep with him."

I tried to change the subject. "I enjoy talking to you."

"Me too."

She was silent for a little while. I sensed how this was a girlish, a womanish, silence.

"Are you patient?"

"If I have to be."

I didn't want to spoil things. She was still testing me. But it was also temptation turned inside out. I tried to calculate how much time we had.

"I've never seen the sea."

"Some camps in Germany are by the sea, like Stutthof. The sea enervates me. I slept through a storm in our cabin by the beach. In the morning I woke up exhausted, as if I'd been sailing all night. It was a storm with rain and wind and high waves. They occur twice a year, around the equinox."

"Teach me to read the cards."

"You probably know what I'm thinking about."

"Maybe."

She got the cards ready. She held up a card with a magician. "You're not guided by logic," she explained.

Some cards signified attributes – bigness, smallness, tallness, darkness, jealousy, haste. Others represented qualities – interest, sadness, bad luck.

Vili had told Leah that, in order to humiliate them and convince them of the pointlessness of their existence, the Greeks had made their enemies tie and untie knots for days on end. The Arabs made their prisoners dig wells and fill them up again. The Romans humiliated their enemies by shaving their heads. The Germans humiliated and tormented their enemies until they welcomed being killed by them. She'd talked about this with Gottlieb Faber. (She didn't know that in the camps in the East the Germans humiliated the women by ordering them to stand naked for hours in front of their huts, including the ones who were having their periods, so that they lost their pride and their dignity, and were left feeling helpless and ashamed, impotent, until even their impotence was extinguished.) Leah's voice was intertwined with the darkness, the stars and the moonlight.

"The Germans are ageing faster than you and me," I said. "They are losing the war. Their days and nights are closing in on them just as they are on us. The earth is getting smaller under their feet."

"They despise everybody who isn't a killer. They have infected us. I don't wish them anything good."

She was looking through the candle flame at me, at the wall, at what was crawling over it, and through the dormer window into the night.

"I feel like I'm at the bottom of a well. Like a bird that can't fly. Like two feet in one shoe. As a child I thought up a story about a girl who fed on light the way children are fed bread. In the dark she turned into a cat, a beautiful one. At night she hunted mice and birds. In the light she was a good girl."

Leah was watching the shadow the moon was casting. I sought with my eyes what I couldn't touch. Her body and her features supplemented the meaning of her words. She caressed me with them. With the colour of her voice.

On the packing crate by her side she laid out 22 tarot cards in three rectangles, numbered cards, four suits: hearts, clubs, spades and diamonds. There was no need to hurry, but I didn't understand why she was putting this distance between us. Before me she set the king of clubs with his sceptre, wearing a greenish gold-hemmed robe, a card with a clown striking a xylophone at one end and a doll touching a small drum at the other. The queen of clubs held her sceptre in a feminine way, like a short dagger, close to her chest. As Leah bent over her cards, the candle's flame was reflected in her hair.

"This is the moment that will change your life. They've made you a coward because you want to live. You cannot or don't want to kill. They've made your life shameful. Your joyful days are behind you."

I closed my eyes.

"What did the cards tell you about Vili?"

"About some people you don't learn much, even if you live with them. I've learned a lot from him. He is generous when it comes down to it. He knows what has worth and what is rubbish. He wanted, or so he says, the best of all worlds for himself and for me. You can judge yourself whether he has succeeded."

During the night from Sunday to Monday, and in every waking moment, I had seen Leah's white belly in my mind and wanted to kiss it. She was looking at my head.

"You're good enough to eat," she said.

I had my own ideas about what she was good enough for.

She was aware of me examining her. I didn't want to talk to her about Vili. Only in part because of jealousy. It occurred to me that Vili didn't seem all that bad to her – or I all that good. They were leaving their furniture behind. What would happen to it? One of their protectors from the Council of Elders would deal with it. I noticed that in fact they'd packed some of their books.

Then she said: "Flesh, hair, fat – that's all we are."

I touched the cards.

Then she said: "You're going to live longer than him or me. You won't know who they're going to kill instead of you."

"What's the most important thing for me?"

"Now?"

"Altogether."

She looked right at me with her attentive blue eyes. "That I don't see in the cards."

"What isn't in them?" I joked.

"Don't ask. Even when you know the difference between good and bad, you still do what you want."

The old people were exchanging rumours about the numbers of prisoners killed and about the Allied and German troops. We could hear every word.

"That old woman – before they moved her in here, she burned all the photographs she had of herself when she was young.

"They say there are 450 kinds of pain."

She touched my hand with the tips of her fingers. Heat surged through me.

When I remained silent, she said: "Be patient."

I wondered how long I would have to be patient.

She swept the cards into a heap, burying the constellations.

"You'll understand before the night is over. At daybreak we'll say goodbye. When we'd slept together for the first time, I felt in the morning as if Vili had carved my heart out of me. He doesn't look for a woman's heart between her legs."

The wind whistled outside.

Light came from the window of the Central Registry; they were still working. They still had enough people to choose from. I breathed in Leah's breath: I had nothing to compare her perfume to. Perhaps plants, paths or fields. The breath of night. Should I tell her how wonderfully she smelled, how pleasant the closeness of her body was?

"Beautiful girls shouldn't get married, my grandmother Olga used to say."

"Why not?" asked Leah.

"I often think about her."

"I can see your grandmother in your eyes."

Then she said: "I'd wanted to become part of Vili's world. I'd hoped he would also deserve me."

"Did he?"

"He taught me what two people can give one another."

"How long do you want to remain grateful to him?"

"Till tomorrow morning," she smiled her porcelain smile.

The old people had fallen silent. The noises of the night were becoming fewer. We could hear birds, dogs, cats and crows in the distance. I wondered when we'd hear the noise of the loco-motives from the shunting yard. We'd heard the clank of the cattle trucks being assembled many times before; this time it worried me. (Actually it had always worried me, except that until now someone else had always left in my place. In whose place would I be leaving?) In my mind's eye I saw the children who before every transport held hands out of fear that they'd get lost. The sky was full of stars. One shot across the heavens.

"Make a wish."

"Made one already," I answered.

The candle was burning down. I wasn't hungry but I knew what hunger might do to us on the journey. The weak and the dying do not rebel. Nor do the frightened.

Leah touched the darkness just as the darkness touched her. Did she feel like a daughter of Theodor Herzl, founder of Zionism? For a second there was almost coldness in her blue eyes, like fishes. She asked me to sing to her. I knew the Czech ballad of the robbers' lover who shielded their chief with her body when the gendarmes attacked their camp. Leah listened to the end.

"At home we had a bathroom with mirrors right up to the ceiling in one corner," she said. "As a child I'd lock myself in and look at myself in the mirrors from all sides. My nose, my profile, my body, my legs, my arms. I examined the differences between the two sides of my face. I wasn't sure what I wanted. My father had an aquiline nose. I inherited – luckily – my mother's nose. I measured my breasts in the mirror. I felt I was flying. Did I really exist? I cried. I verified that I had real tears running down my cheeks. I was afraid my mother might die."

She turned her head. I wished she'd say to me: "Do what you want."

"You can't change much. Unless you're Gottlieb Faber."

Then she asked: "D'you want to do this just the once?"

I didn't know how to answer her. What did she want me to say?

I wondered what would happen to Leah if she didn't go off the next day, if she survived and returned to Leeuwarden.

"I lost my virginity in a wood by a pond, during a thaw. I'd gone to the wood with a boy I didn't really like. We sat on a moss-covered stone. It was early spring, the trees were in blossom, the moss was turning green, and the wood smelled of resin. The birds were singing. Maybe there is beauty in being untouched. In something not yet discovered. In something occurring for the first time. As a child I believed that what's first is best. What is last is pitiful."

The candle had nearly burned down. From the window came

a cold breeze. The moon had changed places with the stars. She was watching the dying flame.

"Of all the books I've ever read or at least dipped into, the Bible is the most truthful. It is about how we fall or how we rise up. How we are capable of being evil to each other. What we are – a deep dark pit or a towering mountain range. About how you never know what you'll do. What others will do."

The candle went out. Only a little puddle of wax was left.

"Perhaps I don't even exist. I just imagine everything," she said.

"You exist when I touch you," I said.

With the tip of my finger I touched the back of her hand.

I thought of her softness, her smooth skin, wrists, hands and knuckles. She drew her hand away. I slid mine down to her fingers. Her fingers were nice and long.

"Not yet," she repeated.

I liked things to be simple. I was colliding with many-sided shields behind which she was hiding.

"It's getting late," I said.

"Yes. If I had an oven I'd bake you some bread for the journey. What a woman likes best to give a man is food."

I didn't understand till later why she had said this. She was offering me something and denying something, giving and taking away at the same time.

It was getting cold. I went to shut the window.

"Can't see anything," I said. "Think that you've baked bread for me," I said. "Thank you." I laughed.

She laughed too. The word *bread* had a strange sound in the attic. It conjured up visions of the harvest, the cycle that begins, ends and continues in the soil. It conjured up the coarse colour of earth, of innocence or aloofness, of indifference. Thousand-year-old notions.

I touched her hand with the tip of my finger. She trembled. Something had changed. In her eyes was the sea with its unfathomable depth, with its unpredictability and intransigence.

I touched her with my palm. She did not resist, she didn't withdraw her hand, but I didn't feel any response. She'd lost her porcelain smile in the dark.

"Would you like me to undress you?" she asked.

I didn't have to answer. I didn't have to think what she preferred and why. I thought of what Vili had done to Ruth Winternitz in Prague, and how she had aroused and provoked him.

"You're not undressing?" I answered her question.

I didn't want to admit that she had caught me off guard and yet not totally surprised me.

"Come with me." She offered me her hand.

Together we went to the bed. Leah undressed me slowly. Her hands were hot. She had no difficulty with my shirt, she only had to undo the last two buttons. She took her things off without hurrying. Her body was just as beautiful as her face.

She asked, almost inaudibly: "Are you also afraid that you'll die old?"

In her voice I heard a yearning with which I identified. A music I hadn't heard before.

I felt like an acrobat hanging from a trapeze, careful not to fall and injure or kill myself. I could hear my heart. I hoped she could hear it too. I was shaking from head to toe. I consisted of body and skin, of breath, anxiety, a thumping heart, trembling and yearning.

"You don't have to tell me," she whispered. "You don't have to say that you love me. A song of love is a sad song."

I was aware of the rain approaching and retreating, coming on gusts of wind, of what makes each night mysterious. Everything began to pass by me, as if I were on a boat sailing into impenetrable darkness. I felt like an animal that senses the presence of a danger which has no voice, face or taste, and the reward for which is pleasure.

She was still whispering. "I'd like to know what love is. Perhaps it's the same for everybody and yet different. Like dusk when it gradually touches night, and like dawn before daylight swallows it up. Men shouldn't just love women for their beauty. What will they do when they grow old?"

I didn't say anything. How could she still talk?

"I know what longing is," she whispered.

The pale moon lit up the strings of rain, the mist and the pre-dawn clouds. Leah from Leeuwarden opened like a white ocean.

"If you don't forget me, I'll always be with you." Hope had returned to her voice. She was still trembling. I embraced her tightly, as if she were freezing.

Then she asked: "Do you want a child with me?"

"This is enough," I whispered. "It's everything."

"It's got to be enough," she said. And then: "Come closer. As close as you can."

"You're like a white and rosy sea," I whispered.

I stroked Leah's face and hair with both my hands, with my 17-year-old soul I caressed her 18-year-old soul. A new kind of beauty was flooding her. She seemed vulnerable in her nakedness. I sought strength in her weakness. The weakness that made her strong. She was like an animal, the animal that is in everyone, an animal that had wandered far away and possibly knew it couldn't come back. It was wonderful and sad at the same time.

She was like a young deer caught. Like a sin for which no-one could be punished. She flooded me like a river. Her golden hair had fallen over her forehead, the hair they would cut off tomorrow or the next day.

The darkness was losing its power. Dawn would break shortly.

"You are beautiful," I said, again.

"You're beautiful too," she replied in a whisper. "Also because you see things as being better than they are. I'd like to be like that. I like you for your ridiculous sense of justice. For how you are warming me as if I were about to freeze."

I never forgot what she said. She allowed me to be proud of myself. I sensed how her body was her own, to do with as she chose.

I heard her exhale sharply and start to cry, and I recalled what Vili had said about her, about the qualities that attracted him to her and which, at the same time, almost expunged what was good in her.

Vili was no longer my role model. I'd had my revenge. I had taken his wife. Or had I simultaneously punished him and forgiven him? I had perhaps just made one of those tiny moves towards adulthood.

"Thank you," I said.

"What for?"

"You're getting rid of everything you don't want," I said.

"What makes you think I don't want it? You're young and

alive," she said, placing her palms on all the spots where she could feel my pulse, my heartbeats, the heaving of my lungs. She was turning into a pearl and a shell, into a garden of intoxicating perfumes, her body had softened into a new shape.

And then she cried and was happy.

Did I want more? Maybe yes, maybe no. And Leah? I've no idea.

The attic recovered its lost dimensions. The moonlight dissolved. Night had turned into day, daylight into movement. Everything emerged into a light without shadows – the boxes, the packing cases, Leah's crocodile handbag, the crate. Two spiders were moving along a beam. Earwigs and bedbugs were crawling over the wall. I tried not to notice them. The bricks had got damp during the night. It was Wednesday.

In my mind's eye I saw an archipelago with a few people. I sensed an equilibrium I'd never felt before.

Then she whispered: "I've heard of civilizations that don't know a higher number than three. Two is all I need. You and me."

I had no answer.

"You're my man," she said.

I was glad she included me among her men.

Not until a few years later did I realize that the Terezín ghetto was where I grew up. I couldn't actually say I had seduced Leah. Only that we'd been together. And what she meant to me, always. I didn't tell her I loved her. I didn't want to lie. I loved her in relation to the time accorded to us.

Suddenly she said: "Friend of my heart."

At that moment I knew what I would have missed if I hadn't been with her.

Music came from the German officers' mess. To them a transport was a joyful event. A harvest festival. Proof of their omnipotence. Leah was listening to the music and to the clanking of the cattle trucks being readied.

The mist outside was white and thick. It was the colour of a mesh from which the holes had been lost.

Leah turned to me. At last she was smiling.

From the tracks, further away, came the sound of a whistle. Again, and a third time.

"I enjoy looking at you," I said.

Her blue eyes were sad.

"The train's assembled," she said. "What they would like best would be for us to kill ourselves, like Gottlieb Faber did."

"You'd better get your things. Two locomotives. Fifty cattle trucks. They don't want us to get stuck on the way."

She was assessing the situation by what she was hearing, like a blind person.

"*Schlussstrich*, as the Germans say. The last line."

She robed herself in light, like trees, rivers or rocks. Flowers before they fade. She put some warm underwear on because it was already cold in the East. I was glad she wouldn't be naked under her clothes.

She regarded me with eyes filled with uncertainty.

"I want you to be strong. To know that you are strong."

"You are strong too," I lied. "Stronger than you think."

At the final moment with Leah from Leeuwarden on that Wednesday morning in September 1944, after a night without sleep, I thought about that secret and art of accepting a person with everything they are and are not, with what they might be and what they never could be, with what they won't say because they don't yet know it, or, if they do, they'll keep it to themselves. What we would be within a few hours' time, on our journey. I thought about how love was born out of nothing, just like stars before they are extinguished though their light continues to shine for us. Maybe love remembered is like the light of extinguished stars.

"It'll be windy," she said.

"You should put on the warmest things you have," I told her again. "Have you got a scarf?"

"I have. But I'll feel naked regardless of what I'm wearing." She touched her hair. "It doesn't matter how thick your scarf is or how warm your boots."

Then she added: "I'd be happy, if you remembered me."

In the morning light of the old people's home near the Firemen's House on L Street in the Great Fortress, Terezín, towards the end of September 1944, next to Leah from Leeuwarden, newly married without having spent her wedding night with her husband, I reflected that one day there would be talk about the different kinds of people who had made it through the war, about those who succumbed at the first onslaught of sorrow, about those who were capable of saying no – to themselves and to those around them – and I also thought about people to whom what I've written would sound contrived and improbable.

"No need to change trains, I hope. And no return ticket. Shall I take my umbrella?" she asked.

"Why not?"

"I still have a girl's umbrella from Leeuwarden. With red and yellow tulips."

"Are you taking your cards?"

"Never go anywhere without them." She smiled.

"They may give you some office job."

"Are you serious?"

"The Germans get rattled when they see someone with flaxen hair, white skin and blue eyes. Suddenly their racial multiplication table is wrong. Your appearance gives you an advantage."

"Of course they'll want to surround themselves with people like me. I've something to look forward to."

Down in the street, hearses drawn by humans were delivering bread and ersatz coffee. The huge wheels with their black spokes rattled and lurched on the cobblestones. (Some of the cobbles were missing.) It was a ridiculous and disagreeable sound until you got used to it. It was a morning sound, the way a cock would crow elsewhere. Triple helpings for those assigned during the night for transport to the East. Most would eat everything at once. (In a little while Adler and I would be among them.) My stomach was grumbling.

Harness straps over their shoulders and round their chests, a dozen men of about forty were drawing the vehicles along, happy they weren't leaving on the transport. They included Leo Baeck, the Chief Rabbi of Berlin, who was wearing his crumpled Sunday clothes, with a tie and elegant shoes. Having refused to become a member of the Council of Elders, he had volunteered for garbage collection. They let him load the refuse, just as I had once done. I recognized him by his cap and his grey woollen scarf.

"The curfew's been lifted. I'd better leave."

"I'm glad you came."

"I'm glad too. See you on the train."

"Or after the war." She smiled prettily.

"It's still misty. But it'll be a fine day."

"I can't believe that we've come to this."

I put my arm round her shoulders. I was trying to breathe courage into her. To get her to set out on the journey with her head held high. I wanted her to be as proud of herself as she was beautiful.

For the first time in my life I said: "Darling."

She looked up. She answered the same way: "Darling."

The word embraced everything. The three or four thousand years we had in our blood. The past few hours we had granted ourselves before our journey. For what would come after us.

Leah turned the key in the lock. She picked up the cases and handed me the ace and queen of hearts. She looked as though she might dissolve in a moment. On her half-open lips was a smile, and in her eyes, as when I'd first seen her, was an eagerness I was unable to explain. At the same time they declared that all was vanity.

I left by the back door. Across the yard, through the broken walls between the blocks, I would manage to get to L 218. Adler would be waiting for me. But before I got round the trough and the latrine, I heard someone turn a big front-door key and the creak of a hinge before the door was slammed.

The old men in the passage asked Vili what was going to happen. As if he knew, as if he was the Almighty. He was exhausted, at the end of his strength. Had the cattle trucks arrived? Were they all cattle trucks, or were there also passenger cars? I recognized his voice. The sky had cleared. It would be better weather for the journey. They were like people drowning, clutching at straws. They were no longer asking to buy themselves out of something or other. Even their illusions were threadbare and false. They called on God. Their God was as powerless and miserable as themselves. I took the shortest route to L 218.

I only learned later what Vili had been doing at the Central Registry that night. He didn't get into the main office. The council employees who were responsible to the Germans for the transport made sure that the boxes of registration cards were under continuous supervision. By then, the leaders knew that in the East there was a chance of life for those whom the Germans allowed to live; after 92 days the chance of survival was one in 29. They knew from eyewitnesses that there were gas, furnaces and, at best, slave labour. Life in the expectation of death, without dignity, without hope. Humiliation, beatings and cold, sickness and hunger. During the selection at the railway ramp, hardly anyone would survive. For nine out of ten, the East meant Zyklon B. Fine green crystals dropped through shower heads. At the same time the leaders were trying to reassure themselves that the East was both a long way away and close to the front, that the Germans were retreating, suffering enormous losses, and that maybe the war would, after all, end one day. They kept all this to themselves so as not to spread alarm, depression or panic. In any case not many people would have believed them. There was nothing the leaders could do. They were victims themselves. It was just a matter of time before their turn would come. The world was like a planet that had left its orbit. There was no point in complaining about the devilish organization of the Germans. Those inside were guided by their own interests, by their drive for self-preservation. The few righteous ones closed their eyes.

Vili had wasted the night. He'd slept in his clothes, only taking off his shoes (even here he'd wear his best and most expensive shoes with crude rubber soles), on the bench set aside for those waiting to do official business, on the third floor of the Magdeburg barracks. He already knew that nobody was taking Leah's place or his. Rabbi Murmelstein had locked himself into his luxury apartment with his Hungarian wife to make sure nobody could call on him with a request. He had too many acquaintances among the men and women who were leaving. And Commandant Rahm insisted that the wheel of destiny should turn without prejudice – at least in his Nazi eyes. This had nothing to do with justice, everything to do with the implacability of the SS. Moreover, Rahm was all for accuracy and invariably inspired a sense of responsibility in both the SS personnel and the Council of Elders. Murmelstein, his Jewish deputy, was not willing to jeopardize his own tenuous safety for the even more tenuous safety of somebody else. What the gendarmes thought of him was a matter of indifference. What mattered were the people in the Commandant's office: SS Commandant Rahm, Hauptsturmführer Heindl, Anton Burger. The German clerks and typists. The staff servants and grooms, the German postman. His life depended on them.

"You wouldn't like me to keep a place for you in the cattle truck?" Adler had wanted to know.

"Sure, the best place in the sleeping car or the dining car."

There was an equilibrium in my soul such as I had never

known before. That amazing feeling of being the first man to exist under the stars. Nothing could upset me. Not even transport to the East.

"We're off, then," I said. "Let's go."

Adler asked no questions. He didn't want to board the train on his own. He was glad I'd come back in time, even if pale from lack of sleep. My whole body ached. I didn't even sit down. We picked up the brown boxes containing our few belongings, and put the strings with our transport numbers round our necks. I was Number 63.

"Yes," said Adler, as if replying to something I'd said. "You never let yourself be detained by details."

"No," I said.

"I remember what you told me, back in Prague, about Flusser – that he wasn't old enough to be stupid."

"I said that?"

"Yes. And that he was born clever, like everybody, and would only get stupid later by adjusting to other people."

"Why are you reminding me of this?"

"So you will think of me like Flusser. Not yet old enough to be stupid."

"Forget it," I said.

"Let's go or we'll miss the fun," Adler said.

So we walked to the station, which cut from the outskirts right into the centre of the fortress, to the longest street, L Street, like a knife into its belly, with a pair of silvery tracks.

"How are you feeling?" Adler asked, finally.

"Fine," I answered. "And you?"

"Also fine. How else?"

"I'd no idea I would stay there so long," I remarked, in an

offhand way. "And you probably have no idea what I've done. And with whom."

"Don't brag," Adler said.

We were in the same truck as Vili Feld. Nobody felt like talking. Everything had happened already. We were leaving the fortress ghetto. We travelled along the valley towards the north, along the Elbe, round the backs of the mountains. The landscape was pleasant and unremarkable, hills and forests, meadows, villages, bridges, small towns. A world no-one could move. September had always been one of the nicest months, better towards the end than during its rainy middle. At least that's what it seemed like to an outsider. It was a world touched only remotely and in- directly by our fate, a world armoured with indifference and silence, with worries about itself. Cut fields, stubble, flocks of crows, swallows, pigeons. A hare running across a field. A pile of potatoes on the platform of a village station we passed without stopping. A soldier by a sentry box with two Great Danes on a long lead. A farm, in its yard a trough full of bran, a dozen pigs with their snouts down. And again woods, mountains, fields of maize and mustard seed. In one little village, a bell was ringing from the church tower. Its sound died away slowly. Mud, greenery, rocks, the tracks going north and then east.

The webs into which the prisoners wrapped their thoughts before leaving their native soil, their former country or the region of their internment, the smell of damp air, thoughts of resist- ance, of freedom. The train moved slowly, the trucks clanked, and the noise of the wheels and the ringing of the rails had a soporific effect. But nobody slept. Everyone's attention was focused on where we were going, on what was going to happen.

Everyone asked themselves the hardest question: is it my fate, when we get to our destination, to survive? Am I prepared to live at someone else's expense, in place of someone else? Am I prepared to swallow my own heart so that, at the crucial moment, my knees don't give way under me? The wheels hammered out a signal everyone understood: survive, survive. We didn't yet know about the rebellion of the *Sonderkommandos* in Auschwitz-Birkenau at Crematorium Number 4, a rising that would take place in a few days' time, when we'd passed through the gate with the notorious inscription *Arbeit macht frei.* (A hundred years earlier, a German had formulated this slogan differently: *Literatur macht frei.*) We didn't yet know about the Warsaw Uprising. About that most noble thing – apart from a conscience – our ancestors had given to the world and to themselves: a measure of freedom and justice, and the prohibition of murder.

The wheels of the train regularly struck the joints between the rails; in some places the rails were bent and the train jumped as if travelling through a vacuum or over an abyss. We travelled along the Elbe, which ran past rocks to the North Sea. We moved from light into dusk, from dusk into nightfall, from nightfall into night. Keeping silent and resting, gathering strength for what lay ahead. The world behind us was vanishing with every revolution of the wheels.

I don't know how to sum up my assessment of Vili Feld. Later, all my judgements and half-judgements seemed misguided. A small pebble in the snow, growing by rolling until it resembles a boulder, a huge ball of snow that triggers an avalanche and buries everything living beneath it. Until the snow melts in spring, and the pebble returns to its original appearance, if somewhat bleached. Vili's ambition, his drive, his will to live when his life hung by a hair. Sometimes he would see himself as a mountaineer who'd just climbed the highest peak because he couldn't survive on the lower ones, and he'd keep his eyes forward so as not to stumble, because the slightest wrong step would cost him his life. He wouldn't pay any attention to others attempting the same peak, but he also didn't know how to climb down because he was seized by vertigo and terror. Was Vili guilty? Not in the eyes of the law. And yet. This "yet" was within him like a shadow no-one saw. And he got away with it every time. Maybe he lulled his conscience the way a father sings to his children to lull them to sleep and, in doing so, falls asleep himself.

Vili Feld was up against stronger circumstances than he could overcome. He asserted himself with passion and, if possible, with elegance, an elegance that reminded him of what he'd been like and what he hoped to return to. He didn't want, and probably didn't know how, to be alone. There were times when even in his best double-breasted suit from the fashionable tailor Barta he looked like a scarecrow, when his clothes hung on him like rags. He'd lost more weight in Terezín than he'd wanted to. He looked masculine, ready to grit his teeth and tighten his belt. To give up most of what he liked. And he prevailed by means of his will, which, however secret or imperceptible at times, was still stronger than that of others. I couldn't deny his tenacity. His intelligence. His acuity, his ability to make quick decisions, most of them correct. I didn't deny his stubbornness, his hardness. Everything was brutal. If he hadn't been brutal himself, he'd no longer be alive.

Vili wasn't the only one who managed to adjust. Everyone knows what that involved. If Adler and I had not adjusted, we'd no longer be alive. As a railway engine hauls wagons, Vili harnessed women to himself. That was what was most special among his specialities. He had qualities that women and young people appreciated. He knew how to listen. He respected others, in spite of everything he did. He also had a purposefulness that was a child of our age. It involved instinct, drive, all the elements of which a man is composed. Passions seemed to dominate him. He drew on the invisible strength of women, even if he was not with them. This was his way of compensating for what had been lacking in his relationship with his mother, who had regarded him as a substitute for his dead older brother. Perhaps. It involved girls of my own generation, little Ruth Winternitz. I never forgave him for that. Perhaps he had once been more disdainful. That had evaporated. He had a courage that sometimes looked like impertinence. But he wasn't arrogant, or he wouldn't have sought or tolerated the company of kids like me.

Adler knew what there was between me and Vili – both sides of the coin, Ruth Winternitz and Leah. It probably seemed trivial to him. Adler believed he knew me like the back of his hand. He was convinced that, in order to function, I had to find an enemy so I didn't regard myself as a sissy. That I was able to discover something hostile even in my best friend. Even in myself. That was my dynamo. To punish others in this way, Adler believed, was a way of punishing myself.

He teased me about this even after the war, but that was still a long way off. He asked me if by any chance I intended to be a judge. As if we weren't all judges, weighing others up, what they had done to us and also to themselves. What they had said or failed to say. What we wanted from them.

In the cattle truck I sensed Vili's presence. He smelled of eau de Cologne, the last of his supply. I knew where he'd got it from. (The best sheepskin, the best furrier.) After a day and a night we would all smell of sweat, after a further two nights of urine. The Germans hadn't bothered to give us drinking water, not to mention water to wash in. They'd put down straw for us. They didn't mind if we felt dirty. We were dirty. We stank the way people stink when they're turned into animals. We were Jews – guilty, without having lifted a finger, of all the crimes, wrongs, diseases and imperfections in the world. If people along our route didn't know the cattle trucks contained humans, they must have concluded, from the stench, that they contained hogs.

Someone said that the girls on the train would be lucky if some of them were assigned to being field prostitutes, either for labourers or for the technical and auxiliary staff. How could he have known?

"The world hasn't changed much," Vili observed on the second morning. His eau de Cologne had evaporated.

We were trying to judge where we were going by watching the telegraph poles go by. Vili's eyes still had that glint of contempt for the world into which he'd been born. The expression of a horseman whose horse had been struck by lightning but who got away safe and sound, merely a bit shaken. Or the owner of a ship lost at sea with all his possessions. The landscape slipping back alongside the train was no longer familiar but had become a strange country. I knew what Vili was promising himself in his mind if by any chance he survived. We were very alike.

Moving in the opposite direction were military trains carrying troops on leave. Our train gave them priority.

"Trans-sport," Vili joked.

The military trains didn't stop. Later we were told that the troops weren't meant to talk to anyone, except among themselves and, later, their families.

Men and women separately. Twenty-five hundred men, twenty-five hundred women. Two locomotives, front and back. Women who during their stay in the fortress had committed minor transgressions like theft or rowdy behaviour, fighting with their Block Elders or among themselves, were in the first three trucks, which were marked in white chalk with the letters "RU" – Return Undesirable – and a cross. The cross didn't need translation. They'd crammed a hundred of us into a truck intended for 40 men or eight horses. We got a place on top of the luggage, under the roof. A little light and some air came in through a wired-up window and, one night when it was raining, a few raindrops. In the middle of the truck and on the floor people nearly went mad in the press. They had neither light nor air. Those along the walls, over the wheels, were thoroughly shaken up. They were in each other's way. For a day and a night they bore it. The second day and night they hated each other. They beat up a man who dared to say that Hitler had had a grandfather about whom his paternal grandmother, Maria Anna Schickelgruber, never spoke and who was rumoured to have been either Johann Nepomuk Heidler or his brother Johann Georg Heidler or a Jewish merchant from Graz by the name of Frankenberger or Frankreither.

We wished each other dead so there'd be fewer of us in the cattle truck. We travelled for three days and four nights. We had nowhere to go to the toilet. It was more unpleasant for those below us. I'd eaten my food for the journey on the first day. I was reminded of marathon runners, who, according to

Adler, in order not to lose time during their run did everything in their trousers. It was a ludicrous version of a marathon, where the runner, when he reached the finish line, died. The train stopped frequently, but nowhere did they give us any water. In the end we stopped for a whole night in Cracow. Around us, on neighbouring tracks, trains arrived and departed, engines were taking on water, people got on and off or changed trains, wheels ground and whistles whistled. A local loud-speaker announced the departure of trains for Berlin, Warsaw and Sofia. To the North Sea and to Danzig. It sounded like a song. A warm, full, rich female voice. It floated over the station like a dream, full of meaning, beautiful as the stars and hard as the soil. I shall never forget that voice, that night or that journey. Then the voice announced the stops of a train to Hamburg-Altona: Dresden, Leipzig, Oberhausen and Bremen, Frankfurt and Wuppertal. It was filled with the world into which others had been born, born correctly, by the right mothers to the right fathers. It carried a different spontaneity, a different freedom, a different tension or expectation.

The women in the front three trucks, including Leah from Leeuwarden, were not even subjected to the selection process at Auschwitz-Birkenau. Down the long ramp, between two lines of Waffen-SS men with dogs on leads, the women – pregnant ones, sick ones, guilty ones and innocent ones – went straight into the gas chambers. Doctors and SS guards merely gestured with their thumbs to show them the way. Most of them had no idea where they were going, or else they merely suspected. Some of them tripped over the rails. Twenty minutes later, they had been poisoned by Zyklon B and consumed by the ovens. All that remained were ashes.